The Sixth Extinction

A meteor strike causes a world-wide chain reaction of destruction. By chance a small group is pieced together and takes refuge deep within the safety of Cheyenne Mountain.

Dennis Schweigert has spent his professional career predicting this very event. But it surpasses even his wildest imaginations.

The President of the United States brings Mr. Palmer, his trusted advisor to the mountain. How can he govern what no longer exists? Can Mr. Palmer find the answers he's been seeking for a lifetime?

General Grabowski finds himself in direct conflict with the mountain base's commander, General McIntyre. With impossible and unacceptable conditions both inside and outside their safe haven, can either man come to terms with their new existence?

Join these survivors along with Dr. Mark Zorbas, psychologist Carmen Fletcher, pop diva Alexis Coffey and trucker Agustin Sanchez as they fight their way into a new reality. And, eventually, a new world.

The Sixth

Extinction

Karl Roscoe

Spruce Mountain Press

Dedication

My wife is crazy. I wrote this book about the end of humanity as we know it and she wanted it dedicated to her.
So I dedicate this bleak book to my crazy wife whom I love more than anyone will ever know.

First printing 2008

Copyright Karl Roscoe/ Spruce Mountain Press © 2008
All rights reserved

Cover and back photography courtesy of NASA

Cheyenne Mountain maps courtesy of globalsecurity.org

This is a work of fiction. The characters and situations in this book are the product of the author's imagination and bear no relation to any person living or dead. Any similarities between the characters and situations to any persons are strictly coincidental.

ISBN 978-0-615-23405-2 (Paperback)

www.karlroscoebooks.info

Acknowledgements

A book is seldom, if ever, a solitary accomplishment. I would like to take a moment up front to thank those people who helped me to write the story I wanted to tell.

First I'd like to thank the folks at the Department of Planetary Sciences at the University of Arizona, Tucson. They have put together a website which allowed me to calculate the exact dimensions of the meteor I needed to whack into the planet. You'll find them at www.lpl.arizona.edu/impacteffects. Be prepared to spend some time there. It took me three days of playing even after I found the rock I wanted. This is a very neat site!

Next I'd like to thank Mr. Bill Bryson for having written A Short History of Nearly Everything. It was through his chapters on Yellowstone that I was able to describe the things that happen here. Not to mention that this is one of my favorite books and that it holds a place of honor in my library....

Finally I would like to thank the many, many people who were forced to read my manuscript in its multiple stages of completion. Their help in editing, proofreading and storyline have been invaluable in creating the book you now hold.

Karl Roscoe

The Sixth Extinction

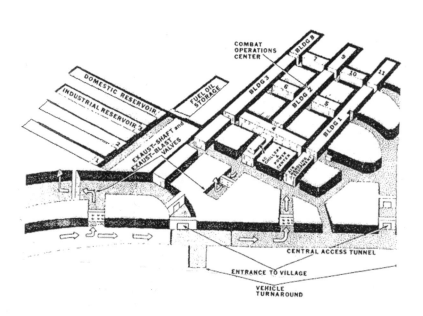

The Sixth Extinction

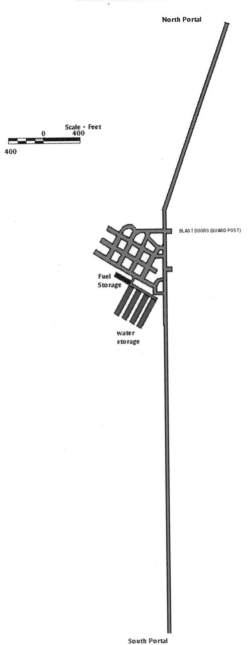

Karl Roscoe

For two billion years the asteroid floated in a grand ellipse around the emerging solar system. It was there to see the creation of the inner planets and the settling and cooling of the star around which they spun. It had found its home on the inner edge of the Kuiper belt, so far away that the sun appeared to be just another bright star. The asteroid was dense and metallic and had forgone the opportunity to fuse with other nearby rocks to become a solid outer planet. Suddenly it was shattered by a comet racing from the Oort cloud towards the inner solar system. The largest fragment, almost two and a half miles across, was pitched out of its orbit and began falling toward the sun. When it encountered the gravity of the gas giants it was slowed. The rock fragment crossed the asteroid belt at the furthest point of its elliptical journey and swung inward toward the inner planets to complete a path around the sun. There, for the next two billion years, it would cross the orbits of Mars and Earth many times; almost but not quite threatening those planets. Then, in a collision with another bit of space debris, there was another slight change in its orbit.

For what seemed like the umpteenth time Dennis Schweigert led a group of twelve freshmen through the jungles of Panama. His close cropped, sandy brown hair and American shorts and hiking boots seemed oddly out of place in the tropical rain forest. He was sleight of build and thin: The kind of thin you get from living too long as a bachelor.

"Si, Santiago, los árboles son muy altos." Jeez, these kids grew up in this country and still they've never set foot in the jungle! "A continuación, vamos a estudiar el ciclo de vida." His Spanish was technically perfect but the accent was hideous. A geologist by trade, he made it plain to anyone who would pay attention—and no-one paid attention after the first time—that he was not happy here. That he did not feel that he belonged here. And that he would leave the moment a teaching position opened in his field and in his country. Unfortunately that had not happened for seven years, and here he was stranded at the Universidad de Panamá, teaching Intro to Biology to rich Panamanian kids. The situation was only made worse by the fact that the Instituto de Geociencias was literally right next door on campus and, having alienated the department head almost immediately with his strongly worded opinions, they had locked him out as soon as he'd arrived.

Dennis Phillip Schweigert was the son of a High School math teacher and a Community College English professor. While he was growing up his parents had always challenged him academically and had taught him to speak his mind and question authority. They both practiced what they preached. When Dennis was a child in the early seventies he was surrounded by the leftover participants of the anti-war and civil rights movements. These activist academics had no qualms about exercising their freedom of speech. Dennis had always considered speaking one's mind to be the norm.

He had done well enough in his rural high school in Idaho to be considered for a coveted slot studying at the Colorado School of Mines. Somehow his parents had scraped enough together to help him stay in college for the first year and his marks earned him a scholarship for the remaining three. He managed to secure a graduate study berth at

UCLA specializing in plate tectonics. He finished his formal education with a PhD from Stanford University. Dennis Schweigert was one of the most promising young minds of his time but he was saddled with the preconception that people would be interested in what he had to say.

And he said. He said that the end was near; that we should prepare as a world. He said that the earth was about to blow to bits; all by itself with no help from political turmoil. He said that asteroids were on collision courses with Earth, that super volcanoes were overdue to blow, that great stores of methane would rise from the oceans and choke out life; that a great calamity was coming to our planet. If we didn't prepare we would be sucked into the maw of history, just as the dinosaurs were. These hysteria-inducing proclamations made him a pariah in the scientific community. Virtually every mind working in the geo-sciences was trying to find a way to predict the next volcanic eruption or subdue the effects of the next seismic event. Having such a loose-cannon colleague bellowing about Armageddon did nothing to enhance their profession in the eyes of the public and would not be tolerated. This is how Dennis Schweigert ended up teaching Biology in Panama and not Geology in the U.S. He could not get hired by any creditable university in the mainstream of education because he spoke out for what he believed. Back in Panama he plodded onward through the dense undergrowth, trying to explain to his distracted students why it was important for them to give a damn about the world that surrounded the world that they lived in. And nobody really listened.

The boulder wasn't much, really. Just another fragment of rock floating through space. Not more than ten tons or so and loafing along fairly slowly through the solar system. Even so, when it collided with the rock fragment it imparted sufficient energy to push it a half degree or so out of its path. That half-degree displacement was just enough to place the asteroid on a collision course with the third planet from the sun.

A dense, metallic, two-and-a-half mile wide, black nightmare now bore down on an unsuspecting Earth. When it hit, it would alter the planet forever.

Karl Roscoe

J ohn Alby had lived in northern Idaho for the past sixteen years. He'd purchased a surplus U.S. military missile silo and it suited his survivalist needs and lifestyle well. John was convinced the end would be coming soon, one way or another.

When he saw the meteor strike the upper atmosphere, he didn't know what it was but he knew it was big. What he didn't know was that, at only two hundred miles from the impact site, the radiation from the fireball would cremate him in less than three seconds. He fell to his knees, his lungs roasting from the inside out. Eighty-six seconds later the earthquake arrived and rocked his lifeless body. As his burnt corpse lay on the flaming ground, he would never know that almost three feet of ash, dust, molten rock and leftover bits of asteroid would cover his remains for eternity.

The asteroid impacted about 25 miles south of Calgary. At its nearly 90 degree angle of impact, it hit the upper atmosphere and immediately began to break up. It took less than two seconds for the pieces to hit the ground. When they struck they created an impact circle just over 4 kilometers wide. Standing 50 miles away from the impact site, the fireball would appear almost 50 miles wide — over 220 times the relative size of the sun — filling the horizon with fire.

The people of Calgary never stood a chance. Their city was simultaneously vaporized from above and rocked by an earthquake from below. The quake measured an unthinkable 9.4 on the Richter scale. The asteroid had carved out a gash 27 miles wide by nine and a half miles deep. Parts of the surrounding land began to tumble into the crater's depths. When the earth was finished crumbling back into the void, a crater remained that was over 44 miles wide and half a mile deep. The sky was black. Ash and debris were falling and would continue to fall for months.

Spokane, Coeur d'Alene and Edmonton were incinerated, the radiation arriving there in tenths of a second after it had swept over John Alby. A minute and a half after impact, earthquakes rocked these cities and tore them apart. Buildings cracked, stucco peeled off the sides and crashed to the ground, underground pipes burst and rail lines bent like saplings. Trees spontaneously burst into flame; fires were everywhere. All life was wiped out within minutes. When the ash began to fall it covered this gruesome scene almost mercifully. In the end, these cities were buried under thirty-three inches of soot.

It took a little longer for the effects to reach Seattle, Portland and Boise. For those who were looking, the fireball appeared eight times larger than the sun. The radiation lasted almost two minutes and burned their faces and exposed skin like a bad sunburn. Then, almost three minutes after impact, an earthquake rumbled through, toppling dishes, breaking windows, cracking walls and causing cars to rock in the street. It was four inches of ash that fell in these cities.

Finally, a thousand miles away from the impact site, in Denver, Salt Lake, Sacramento and San Francisco, two hundred and forty-one seconds after impact, the earth wobbled and swayed. Dishes rattled, a few windows were broken. People turned their heads and wondered aloud: "What was that?" Later an inch of ejecta would cover their homes.

Karl Roscoe

"Mr. Vice President, we've lost contact with Air Force One." The pallid aide was immobile as she reported the grim news.

"You sure it's not just a glitch or something?" said the Vice President. "This happens fairly regularly." He impatiently glared at the woman, obviously eager to get back to the meeting she had so abruptly interrupted.

"We're quite certain, sir." She held his gaze evenly while she spoke. "I think you'd better come with me, sir. This is really big." She stepped away from the open door and made an inviting gesture.

"Goddamn better well be important," fumed the Vice President. "Please excuse me," he said to his guests. "This shouldn't take long at all." He stepped out through the door toward which the aide had gestured. Turning to her he snapped, "Now just what the hell is this about?"

She pointed in the direction of the banks of televisions, all depicting the scene of some terrible calamity: Some in Seattle, some in Portland, two in Sacramento and a few scattered feeds coming in from minor markets in the west. "We don't have any idea what has happened yet, sir. Something knocked out the power grids all over the northwest. Numerous cities are completely blacked out—no communications at all. That includes Spokane, sir: The last stop on the President's fund raising tour."

The Vice President thought for a moment. "Who do we have up there? Mountain Home? Fairchild?"

"I've spoken with the Pentagon. Fairchild isn't responding. Mountain Home, as well as the Boise news outlets, are reporting an intense flash to the north, followed by a pretty sizable earthquake. Power availability is spotty so big picture communications are difficult. We have to rely on the few sources we can contact."

"Russians?" mused the VP.

"Not likely, sir. They're reporting that their seismic sensors have picked up a massive event in Canada—around Calgary. We're trying to get in touch with the Prime Minister now but she's pretty overwhelmed. Calgary isn't responding and neither is Edmonton. Like I said, sir, this is big."

"Get the staff into the situation room. Keep trying to locate the President."

"Yes, sir," she said crisply, and broke off into a trot.

Karl Roscoe

Dennis Schweigert sat in his office contemplating the blackness that was to be his future. On the wall hung a framed quote. It said simply, "LIFE WILL." The bookshelves were neatly stacked with years of collected journals, textbooks and half-written arguments. On the desk in front of him lay recent editions of *Science, American Mineralogist* and *Geology*. His work was not featured in any of them.

There was a commotion in the hall outside and it sounded as though it was coming in his direction. "Dennis, Dennis!" came a multitude of voices. "Idaho is on fire! There was an earthquake! Something has happened!" Five colleagues burst through his doorway and descended on him, all speaking at once. "Idaho, Dennis! Look at the cable news!" It was a cacophonic mixture of English and Spanish but their urgency was enough to cause him to act immediately.

He spun in his chair and turned on the small TV he had in his office. Not needing to change the channel (he only watched the cable network) he was horrified to see rescue crews pushing through inches of ash; destruction rampant everywhere. The announcer was breathlessly describing the scene at one after another of the cities and towns in utter rubble. "Calgary is gone," he was saying. "It would appear that a massive volcano, previously unknown to geologists, has exploded virtually underneath the city. Every city and town within two hundred and fifty miles has had all life wiped out. The death and damage toll is staggering...literally inconceivable."

Schweigert stood, shaking his head. "I've got to get back there," he said. He grabbed his glasses off his desk and strode for the door. "My parents...my sister...." He paused for one moment at the door and said, "Estella, can you cover my classes?" Then he was gone down the hall. He had left his cell phone on his desk. It would later ring, unanswered, with a Washington D.C. number in the caller window.

Gina Trower had moved to Hawaii ten years ago in search of the perfect wave. She had grown up in southern California, mostly on the beach. She was lucky enough to have found a lucrative modeling contract which had allowed her to travel extensively and work on her surfing credentials. She'd been on the world tour since she was nineteen and was more at home in the water than out.

When she was twenty-three she moved to Australia for the waves but had been somewhat put off by the sharks, jellyfish and other spiny and poisonous critters. The waves were some of the finest in the world but the hassle of the wildlife had caused her to search for better places to live and surf. After two years she packed up and dropped anchor in Hawaii.

She'd been out all morning trying to find good waves but the surf was not cooperating. She had just finished riding a mediocre four footer and was paddling out in hopes of finding one decent wave before lunch when she heard a commotion coming from the people on shore behind her. Turning and sitting up on her board she saw a crowd pointing out at the ocean and shouting excitedly. A few were breaking out into a run back toward the island's center. Thinking it was just another tour ship out there, she spun back to her belly-on-the-board paddling posture. After the first few strokes she lifted her head to scan the horizon for a surfable wave. At first she didn't understand: There was no horizon. Only ocean rising above her. Feeling the first shivers of the excitement of a coming big wave, she brought one knee up and looked higher. Then higher. Then higher still. The wave was beginning to curl 100 feet above her head; its base was just arriving at her position in the water.

"Ah, hell," she thought, "If I'm gonna die, it may as well be on the baddest wave to ever hit Hawaii..." and she rose and steered her board toward an intercept course with the monster tsunami.

Agustin Sanchez finished filling out the paperwork on the generator unit now strapped to the trailer attached to his rig. It was a used Freightliner but it still had plenty of life in it, and it was his. He'd been working on getting a tractor of his own for thirteen years and he'd finally saved enough money to buy this one earlier in the year. The trip would be his seventh with it and he was enjoying driving immensely.

"That'll do it, buddy," said the man at the loading dock. "You sure you know how to get to Salt Lake?"

Agustin smiled, playing along, though he was tired of it. "Si, señor. I am now a ceetizen," he said, heavily stressing his Mexican accent. "I can drive aneeewhere now!" He was poking fun but the man was unaware of it.

The dock worker looked doubtfully at him. "Yeah, whatever. This thing needs to be in Salt Lake...that's SALT LAKE CEEETY by Saturday. Comprendo?"

Agustin sighed. Do all these people think just because you look Mexican that you are incapable of navigating America's highways? "Si, Salt Lake," he repeated. "Saturday, muy bueno." He didn't bother to tell this person that he lived in Salt Lake and had for fifteen years. He climbed into the cab of his truck and started the engine. This was the best part. No badgering dock workers, no condescending middlemen, nobody to hassle him. Just Agustin, the open road and his beloved rig, together. And by Friday night he'd be home in Salt Lake with his wife and three children. Gunning the engine out of the parking lot he drove through the Florida haze, heading north for home.

Ed Beidelmann had been going nuts for eighteen hours. Something immense had happened about a thousand miles away and it had the signature of something he should know about. Ed was the Department Head of Earth and Space Sciences: Geology, at the University of Washington, Seattle. Unfortunately, whatever that something was had blanked out the power that supplied many of his sensors and receivers in the area. Washington D.C. had been on the phone for him three times in the last twelve hours and the last time had been the office of the brand new President. He had used up just about all of his resources when he thought of Hiroki.

Hiroki Nagamachi was the Director of Seismology, Seismology and Physics of the Earth's Interior Department at the University of Tokyo. He had initiated a joint study program with Beidelmann two years ago that involved a second set of sensors relayed directly to Tokyo. If these sensors were still active, he could get a near-real-time readout of whatever it was that had happened and finally get some answers for Washington.

Although phone service was spotty and unreliable still, he called the local provider and dropped the President's name with the head honcho. This was enough to secure him a line to Hiroki. Now if he could just get him to answer. He was lucky; on the first try he got through to one of Hiroki's grad students. The kid volunteered to personally deliver the man in question. When he came to the phone Hiroki was extremely agitated and began speaking almost immediately.

"Massive, Ed. Just absolutely massive!"

"Yeah, we've figured out that much from where we're sitting. What exactly are you showing, Hiroki?"

"This thing is unbelievable! Epicenter is about 20 or 30 miles from Calgary. There was nothing there—flat readings: Then an almost instantaneous 9.4. It's impossible, Ed! These things just don't explode out of nowhere with no warning."

"So what theories are you working right now? Unknown fissure? New super volcano? Extension of known faults? Pressure spot? What the hell is this, Hiroki?" Beidelmann was nearing desperation.

"You might want to sit down for this, Ed" began Nagamachi. "Our best working theory is a meteor."

"Meteor?! Christ, we've got so much space crap up there collecting data, we should see one of those months away! I don't think the signature on this looks like it could be a space rock. What else have you got?"

"Look at the facts, Ed. There's no mapped geology. No reason for an explosive fault. In fact, we have no precedent for this kind of activity without prior indications. The earth just doesn't let go with a 9.4 quake without even a tremor to announce its intentions." There was a short silence as Beidelmann digested the information. "I'll e-mail what I've got right now and keep the feed open," continued Nagamachi. "Do you have access to a computer? How's the power situation there?"

"Right now it's crap," sighed Beidelmann. "Lines are down everywhere. Whatever it was did some major damage before it got to us." Beidelmann thought for another moment and then said, "Send me what you've got and we'll try to find an untied line. Thanks, Hiroki. I mean it. We're getting quite a bit of pressure to identify this thing. Your data's going to help a lot."

"Good luck, Ed. Stay safe over there, OK?"

"I'll be in touch. Thanks again." Beidelmann hung up thoughtfully. "Meteor," he mused. "Meteor!" He shook his head and thought, "I'll be damned!" He called his grad students and professors together and began an impromptu brainstorming session. He also got hold of a few of the astronomy professors to augment the team. He wanted to have one hell of a package built. And when the presentation was ready, it was going to be a fairly stunning phone call to the President of the United States.

Carmen Fletcher was on her ninth patient that hour and was testy as hell. Injured people and their relatives kept pouring into the small hospital, as though Casper, Wyoming was a major metropolitan center. The last two had come from Gillette; more than 100 miles away. They babbled about the rampant destruction they had witnessed as she tended to their wounds. "Tend to their wounds," she snorted to herself. "God's sake, I'm a psychiatrist! I've only got an M.D. so I can prescribe meds to crazy people. I can't even remember my internship, let alone how to splint a compound fracture properly."

And yet she persevered, pushing herself from injury to injury. It was beyond conception. Car accidents, broken limbs, fractures, gashes, burns, eye injuries, concussions. It was like the season finale for a bad TV medical drama, only it was happening here in her own backyard. Here was one with a skull fracture and probable concussion. That one obviously had a broken leg. Next to her was a teenager with a sickening burn over about 30% of his body. Moans filled the room. The hospital staff had begun filling the beds, then cots and finally, floor space. There was now so little room in the hospital that they had begun looking outside for other options. The parking lot was unacceptable. Ash continued to fall like February snow outside and had piled up to two inches already. Several businesses had offered their lobbies and reception areas but, even as those filled to capacity, still the injured came.

"Holy crap!" thought Carmen, "I didn't know there were this many people in all of Wyoming, let alone just around this town!" She knew that this line of thinking was a defense mechanism she was employing to keep herself from losing it. She had to. No one could possibly transition from mundane day to day existence to the insanity and drama of a battle field without so much as a word of warning. There she had stood, in line at the apothecary when a "whump" passed by outside. Several people wandered out of the waiting area to investigate. Most had decided that they had imagined it when the quake rolled through. Casper was not a town built for earthquakes and began showing signs of strain immediately. Brick houses cracked along mortar lines, some walls rocked and fell. There were a few car accidents caused by the waves coursing through solid earth. Pictures fell from walls injuring those sitting below. Many people fell down stairways as the ground pitched and rocked.

She had stepped over near the plate glass windows by the entrance to watch with the curious when the rocking started. She swayed first one way, then abruptly stumbled in the opposite direction. There was an explosive crashing noise as the plate glass gave way in front of her. A little boy about three years old was standing with his hands on the glass when it shattered. Long saber-like shards dropped from the ceiling onto the people standing beneath. Carmen watched as the mother, struggling against the rolling earth, had witnessed the sheets of glass slice across the child's body. His gut was split wide open. Shock and disbelief flared in his frightened eyes as he saw his own entrails spill out in front of him. Then a huge sheet slid across him from above, opening his carotid artery. He was effectively dead as his little body hit the floor. The mother's scream blended in with all the rest.

That was the first death Carmen had witnessed in the last day and a half but by no means the last. The morgue was filled to capacity and other areas were soon recruited to serve. Corpses were unceremoniously left alone in storage closets while rooms were overstuffed with the injured. The enormity of death was everywhere. Somewhere in the back of her mind she was calculating that it would take months — perhaps even years — to overcome the trauma that all of these people had beheld on this day. And she was silently wondering what mechanisms she would employ to handle the Post-Traumatic Stress Disorder she knew that she herself would be combating.

Power vanished during the earthquake but in this part of the country generators were plentiful. Their roar outside accompanied the moans inside. Extension cords snaked everywhere. Those who were not injured stood by ready to help. That was one welcome hallmark of central Wyoming: Where there was a need, there was a community there to fill that need. Gas station attendants volunteered all the gas you could pump to fill the generators. Farmers brought in hay trailers to transport the wounded. Ranchers offered butchered animals to feed all the people. Everywhere she looked there were eager hands waiting to be told how to help.

There was someone behind her, placing hands on her shoulder and waist. "This way, honey," said a female voice. She turned her head to see a motherly woman guiding her out of the hospital and onto the street.

"Emma?" she said.

"That's right, honey. I think two days without sleep is just about enough for you. There're others to take care of these folks. You need to take care of yourself right now."

Emma was her adoptive mother. Her parents had died when she was in college. Emma had stepped in for them and became her best friend and advisor. This was about the most welcome thing that could have happened at that moment. She melted against Emma's warm, soft frame. It was the next best thing to having her own mother right here.

"Emma, there are so many..." she started.

"Yes there are, Carmen. And there will be plenty more when you get back here." Emma was loving but firm. "Right now I want you to come back to my house and get some rest."

Carmen allowed herself to be guided to the car. She welcomed the thought of escape into the emptiness of sleep. The thought of escape from the nightmare that had become her world.

Karl Roscoe

Dennis Schweigert paced nervously through the halls of the Colorado Springs airport. He had caught a TACA flight from Panama City to Mexico City, connected on American through Dallas and hopped on the Colorado Springs flight in his desperate efforts to get to Idaho. Anything, anyway to get north. Always north. Now, after 27 hours of travel time, he was grounded. In fact, all air travel was grounded in the northern half of the United States. The ash cloud had blown halfway across the Atlantic and was continuing to drift eastward. Flights to the west coast had been cancelled due to the possibility of flaming out jet engines at altitude. Watching the ash drifting around the immobile airplanes outside and mulling over his options for ground travel, he heard a loudspeaker paging his name.

Finding the legendary white courtesy telephone he was stunned to hear a voice on the other end ordering him to stay where he was and wait for an army escort.

"Excuse me, General..." he began.

"It's not General, sir. It's Staff Sergeant. Sergeant Gibbons, sir. General Grabowski asked me to call and advise you he'd be wanting to speak to you as soon as we can get a staff car over there. Welcome to Colorado, sir. It seems you'll be spending some time with us here at the 'Mountain Post'."

"Bullshi..." began Schweigert when he felt a hand at his elbow. A young army soldier stood easily at his side.

"Mr. Schweigert? This way please, sir." He offered to take the phone from Schweigert's hand and replaced it on the receiver. A disbelieving and sleep deprived Dennis Schweigert watched the soldier as if in a dream. The young man guided Schweigert calmly and escorted him toward the exit. Dennis allowed himself to be led to a waiting olive drab sedan outside.

"How the hell did you find me so fast?" he asked.

The driver chuckled. "Kinda like something you'd see in the movies, isn't it sir? Truthfully, it's no big deal." He shrugged his thin shoulders and said, "I was just calling the motor pool to let them know my scheduled pickup wasn't going to be able to make it in. My dispatcher asked me to try to find you. Actually you sort of stuck out, so it wasn't that hard. I guess it's not so much fun when you take the mystery out of it, is it?"

"Mmmm," responded Schweigert, suddenly feeling the effects of his extended travel.

The driver checked his rearview mirror. "Sir, it's about a twenty minute drive.... Maybe you'd like to catch a bit of shuteye."

"Doesn't sound like such a bad idea," he responded. His exhausted body overcame his worried mind and in only seconds he was deep in the grip of slumber.

Karl Roscoe

T he year was 1961. Four years after the Soviets had launched Sputnik I, John F. Kennedy found himself enduring Khrushchev's public shoe pounding and the humiliation that was the failed Bay of Pigs invasion. The United States' risk of attack from Soviet ballistic missiles was underscored by the soon-to-occur missile crisis with Cuba. Defense was on the minds of all Americans and something had to be done.

An audacious plan had been hatched to protect U.S. offensive capability: Dig a four acre facility 2000 feet beneath the protective cover of a granite mountain. Thus was born the North American Air Defense Combat Operations Center deep within the bowels of Colorado Springs' Cheyenne Mountain.

Over the course of the next three years, miners bored a tunnel almost a mile long through the mountain. To one side of this tunnel they excavated three chambers, each 45 feet wide, 60 feet high and almost 600 feet long. These chambers were intersected by another four. These measured 30 feet wide by almost sixty feet high; each of them over 330 feet long. Within these caverns engineers erected a small city. In all, fifteen freestanding buildings were constructed: Twelve of them stood three-stories tall. To maintain immunity from a nuclear blast, the buildings were connected by flexible vestibules. There beneath those hundreds of tons of rock, engineers constructed an indestructible military control center.

It took two years to complete construction of the base which was finally completed in 1966. The heart of the station was the Combat Operations Center; a three story building resting atop 1,319 one-thousand-pound steel springs. This design gave the building the ability to flex up to 12" in any direction in the event of a direct nuclear hit. Cheyenne Mountain could boast the amenities of any modern military base, including a chapel, a small exchange, a two-bed infirmary and a pharmacy, a dining facility and even a dental clinic. Because it was designed to be a stand-alone facility, it held water in four immense reservoirs with a total capacity of 1.5 million gallons. Primary electrical supply came from the city of Colorado Springs but was supplemented by six monstrous diesel generators. Overall the facility was designed to accommodate over 1000 people.

Because it was originally conceived as a shelter from a nuclear explosion, the complex was isolated from the tunnel, and therefore the outside, by a pair of 25 ton steel blast doors. The Combat Operations Center was quite secure in its cavern behind that protective shield.

The original situation room in the center looked very much like NASA's mission control from the Apollo days. Over the years it was updated and, at the start of the new millennium, consisted of a number of desks set in a room with flat-panel displays providing up to the minute information.

By July of 2006, most of the functions of the mountain base had been taken over by operational units at nearby Peterson and Schriever Air Force Bases. Cheyenne was renamed as a directorate and placed in a "warm standby" status. It retained the ability to be brought up to fully operational capability within a matter of a few hours. So it was that within 12 hours of the meteor's impact the order had been given and Cheyenne was brought back to life.

Karl Roscoe

"Quickly children. Your father will be hungry and we need to bring him lunch!" Leah Sandon bustled about her kitchen in their small home in Security, Colorado. Jacob, the eldest, helped round up the lunch things for his father while Joshua bundled the twins into their car seats for his mother. Leah finished combing seven year old Ruth's hair and called, "Time to go! Everybody in the car!" The children obediently piled into the family's minivan, Jacob carrying Ezekiel, one of the twins; Ruth carrying the lunch basket and Leah carrying Rebecca, the other twin. Their drive to Cheyenne Mountain was a quick 15 minutes, punctuated by a few coughs from their used and tired vehicle.

"Lord," prayed Leah, "please let us make it so he doesn't have to suffer any hunger." These prayers were as automatic as breathing for her. "Please hold this car together for us, Jesus. Thank you, Lord."

"Thank you, Lord," came a chorus of small voices from the back seats.

At a nondescript desk in a building within the Cheyenne Mountain complex, a buzz came from Caleb Sandon's telephone. "They're here, Captain."

"Thank you, Sergeant" replied Sandon. "I'll be right out." Sandon began the long trek that would take him to the entrance of the military base. It was about ten minutes to walk through the facility to the entrance where he could meet with his family. This was a daily occurrence for the Sandon family. Leah and the children would pack up a lunch for them all and drive over to feed the father at his place of business.

"Daddy!" shouted the children when he strode into view.

"Praise God!" returned Sandon, looking to the heavens. "Thank you for providing me with such a loving family!"

"Praise his holy name," said Leah kissing her husband lightly on the cheek. "How's your day?"

Sandon grimaced. "Nobody knows anything for certain. Our satellites are all blinded in the northwest. Power outages, no communications capability and they still haven't figured out what it is for certain. I guess you know what I think...."

"But all those people—what kind of sin could be so great?"

"The sin of man, Leah," he answered matter-of-factly. "God's time has come. Armageddon has begun. And we will be among the chosen who will ride with Jesus to be with the Holy Father."

She held tight to his arm and moved closer. He was, of course, right. He was always right. Caleb was the smartest Christian she had ever met and marrying him was the smartest thing she had ever done. "Are you hungry?"

"Starved!" he said. "I've been on the phone with important people all over the country today, trying to sort out this mess. Until He comes, I still have a job to do for our country."

She smiled and admired this man anew. She loved him so much.

Karl Roscoe

The newly-sworn-in President was more irate than he had been in the three days since his predecessor had been incinerated in Spokane. It would be many weeks before he would be comfortable in his new position. He still had to choose a Vice President amid all the calamity that was going on in the west. He felt as though he hadn't slept in a month. His aides were all skittish and jumpy. In fact, all of Washington was on edge.

"Where the hell is this Schweigert clown, dammit?" he growled.

"We've finally located him, Mr. President. He's with General Grabowski at Fort Carson. Colorado Springs, sir."

"So why isn't he *here?*" inquired the President, pointedly.

The Chief of Staff spoke up. "Mr. President, all flights have been grounded. The ash is chewing up jet engines all over the northern half of the continent. It just doesn't make sense to try to fly him here."

The President rubbed his eyes. "OK, how do we get direct communication with this guy? I want to talk to him face to face."

The Chief of Staff looked around the room. A helpful aide spoke up. "Sir, we can fly out to Omaha pretty safely. That's about 100 miles south of the ash cloud, particularly if we approach from the south. We could take off from D.C. and head for Little Rock and then jog back to the north. I think that should be pretty safe. After that it's an eight hour drive from Colorado Springs. We could have him waiting for you at Offutt Air Force Base."

"No," said the President, "no. He's just fine where he is. If you think it's safe enough, I'd like to fly out there." The new President sighed, the mantle of leadership weighing heavily upon him. "A personal visit to the west is about in order right now."

"May I ask sir:" began another aide, "Why is it so important to talk to him? I mean, aren't there about a thousand good meteorologists we can ask about this?"

The Chief of Staff glared at the questioner. "*Because*, Mr. Palmer, nobody else in the scientific community has written eleven books on the topic. Because nobody else in the scientific community would even go near the subject. And because, Mr. Palmer, even after suffering professional isolation and ostracism, he has continued to publish on the topic. Right now there is only one person on the planet that the President needs to speak with and that person is Mr. Dennis Schweigert."

"Incidentally, for those who don't already know," said the Chief of Staff with a withering glare directly at Mr. Palmer, "*meteors* are a subject quite apart from the weather." The aide shrunk in his chair and stared at the pencil bouncing nervously in his hands. "Now, Mr. President," he continued, "barring any more questions, we'll have him waiting for you in Colorado Springs."

The President sighed. "Thank you, Ted. Something tells me that Cheyenne Mountain might turn out to be a good place to be. Now let's go over all of this from the beginning."

With a wave of a hand the Chief of Staff indicated he wanted transportation as they had discussed. Another aide ran promptly from the room to make the necessary travel arrangements. He then motioned to a senior staffer and said "Margaret, why don't you just do the whole thing for us."

Margaret rose and, somewhat self-consciously, began. "This past Tuesday, at 10:38 AM, Pacific Daylight Time, an asteroid entered the Earth's atmosphere and impacted twenty or thirty miles south of Calgary, Canada. NASA has corroborated that it was a meteor—they have tracking data for the last 40 seconds prior to impact. Professor Beidelmann in Seattle has data on the impact itself: The meteor dug a 45 mile wide crater around ground zero. He tells us that the kill range was up to 200 miles away from the impact site. That included Calgary, Edmonton, Boise, Coeur D'Alene, Missoula and..." she looked down, "Spokane and Air Force One." There was a moment of self-conscious silence in the presence of the newly-inaugurated President. She continued quickly. "The earthquake that followed shook everything out to about a thousand mile radius. The shock caused a shift in a fault off the west coast which created a tsunami. Hawaii was hit by a 100 foot wall of water and it has taken out everything along the islands' coasts. Anchorage, Juneau, pretty much all the coastal Alaskan towns have been wiped out by similar waves. Communications seem to be down all over the place. Even Europe is reporting outages. Initial predictions say that it's going to get dark and cold for a while. Perhaps as long as a month. Essentially the whole world is suffering from the direct effects and we expect it'll be a while before things return to normal. Months is our best guess. Worst case: A year."

The President shook his head. "Alright, I want a top-down review of what and who we have in place. We need a concrete plan to recover. You have until tomorrow morning when I leave for Omaha. Any questions?" The room was silent. "Fine. Get to work."

A lexis Coffey was pissed. Her private jet from New York had encountered engine problems over western Kansas and the pilots had set down in Colorado Springs. *Idiots*! They were saying something about engine fires and emergency shutdowns but she hadn't seen anything of the sort out the window. They were just chickenshits who didn't want to fly any more. Now, after deciding to ride First Class in a commercial airliner, she discovered that there were no airplanes flying anywhere in the west. Something about that stupid volcano in Canada. *God,* didn't they realize that Hollywood's hottest property had to get back to home base to work out the details of her next hundred-million dollar grossing film? Seriously, her Malibu canyon home had been empty for almost two weeks on her latest publicity tour and she needed to water her plants. *And* find out who's been sleeping with who back in L.A.

So now she was trapped in this stupid little nothing airport, with little insignificant peon people chattering and pointing every time she went to the bathroom. No VIP lounge or anything! On her fourth trip back down the length of the small terminal for yet another lap, she brushed past a rumpled looking man being escorted by a soldier. A *real* soldier. She'd never seen one in real life — only the actors paid to play dress-up for her movies. She made a face when she looked at her sleeve where the man had brushed her. She would have to give this shirt to a friend when she got back home.

For the twentieth or thirtieth time that day she dialed her agent's number on her cell phone. For the twentieth or thirtieth time that day her agent answered cheerfully: "Hey baby, how are you getting along?"

"God dammit Jeffrey, you know perfectly well how I'm getting along. Like HELL! What are you doing to fix this?"

"I'm trying, honey but I think I've got some bad news."

"Jeffrey..." she said in a warning tone.

"Sorry baby, but I'm being told that nobody is flying out west now. Nobody. I heard the President himself can't get past Omaha."

"Who cares about the stupid President, Jeffrey? Don't

they know that there are genuinely important people who have a need to travel?!"

"Honey, nobody knows that better than me but right now they just won't listen to reason. It looks like you're going to be there for at least a couple of days."

"A couple of days?!' she whined. "What the hell am I supposed to do in this sorry excuse for a town for a couple of days?"

"Here's what I've done for you," he said as if striking up a contract negotiation. "There's a limo out front to take you to the Broadmoor Hotel. It's the best five-star in town. I'm trying to book some PR appearances for you locally. There's a lot of military there; maybe we can squeeze something out of that. You know?"

"Jesus Jeffrey, I don't know about all this!"

"You be strong for me, sweet-cheeks. We'll get through this thing together somehow. Oh, I've got a call coming in. It's from Sparks: Gotta take this one! Love you! Kiss, kiss!"

She glared at the phone in her hand. "Freak!" she fumed and flipped it shut. Then she began the process of collecting all her bags. "Skycap! Can't somebody help me with all this crap?" Immediately several of the stranded passengers began to collect her many bags to assist her out the door.

Karl Roscoe

The news continued to get worse. Ed Beidelmann was watching the slender needles sketch sharp peaks on the barren paper. The seismographs, brought back to life with the restoration of power to the university, were jumping like Mexican beans. Each was recording micro quakes happening all over the northwest. Mount Rainier, Mount Hood, St. Helens, Mount Baker and everywhere in between was alive with seismic activity. The meteor had let something loose in the Earth's crust and it looked as though it was going to be a very unpleasant future.

"See that one there?" he pointed to a spike in the track. "That's the north flank of Rainier. Seems to be a lot of pressure building on that side."

His colleague nodded. "We're starting to see what

looks like a rift building between St. Helens and Rainier."

"A rift?" queried Beidelmann. That didn't fit with anything he knew about the geology of this area. And no one knew the northwest as well as he did. "That's not right. We're talking about two distinct domes here; there's no link between them."

"*Used* to be no link, Ed. Look at this." The young seismologist pointed to a nearby computer monitor. "I think that it's giving us a fairly clear indication of a connection we never detected. It appears to be a growing lava tube joining the two domes."

Beidelmann shook his head in disbelief. This was contrary to everything he had ever studied about the northwest. He had planned to use everything he'd ever learned to make some rational predictions for the Washington D.C. crowd but these data were turning a career full of notions on its head. "Can we even model this thing when it lets go?" he asked.

"I've got four grad students and the entire computer sciences department working on it right now," was the reply. His face was grim. "Ed, we've got a whopper here and maybe not enough time to evacuate."

Beidelmann winced and held his fingertips to his temples. "I've got to call Washington with another report. I suppose we'll have to call the mayors in Seattle and Tacoma to give them a heads-up. Other than 'watch out,' I can't even imagine what to tell them. I hope to God they have some ideas."

Karl Roscoe

A̲gustin Sanchez was making excellent time. In only two days he had driven from northern Florida all the way to central Nebraska. Only about one and a half days more and he'd be with his family again. The roads were starting to get dusty from the ash fallout from the meteor. The further west he drove, the darker the skies. It looked to him like a large storm was brewing. The other drivers who used the CB radio (Agustin preferred just to listen) were talking about how the northwest was impassable. Wyoming, Idaho, Washington state and western Montana were covered in the fine gray dust which was getting into everything. Diesel motors were getting clogged with the stuff. It got into the air intakes and choked filters, it gummed up the oil and fuel inlets and the fine coating of dust caused brake pads to lose effectiveness. Truckers were on the radio warning each other to take it very, very easy on the road. He was glad he didn't have to go any further west than Salt Lake. It didn't look like he could have even if he'd wanted to.

His plan had been to take I-80 from his present location straight into Salt Lake but the slowing cars ahead suggested he may be finding an alternate route. After a half hour of wading through stop and go traffic, he found himself nearing the source of the congestion. A state trooper was turning everyone back to find other ways to continue westbound. The ash had blocked the highway ahead and stalled vehicles littered the road. There was no getting through on this route. Agustin would have to find another way. He remembered that just a couple of miles back, near Grand Island, there was an exit for state highway 281, a south-bound secondary road. He could take it south to I-70 and continue through Denver.

"That'll probably add another half-day," he thought "but at least I can still make it home." He turned his rig around at a turnout and began backtracking. Another half-day but he was determined to make it to his family by nightfall of the day after tomorrow.

Sheila Sokolowski was worried. In her twelve-year tenure as one of four staff geologists at Yellowstone she'd seen some pretty odd stuff. Geysers erupted from places where no geyser had been before. 200 degree Celsius pools opened in fields overnight. Earthquake induced slides and avalanches happened throughout the park on a regular basis but this was new. After the meteor had hit, Yellowstone had begun shaking like it had Parkinson's disease. A new tremor or temblor hit on an average of every sixteen minutes. Visitors, already spooked by the black skies and the ever present dust, had left in droves. Even the local press people were too busy worrying about what was going on in their own lives to care much about a few earthquakes in a park known for its volatility.

Sheila was worried because she knew, perhaps better than any other human being, that it was time. Every six hundred thousand years (give or take a few thousand) Yellowstone National Park would become the world's largest volcano. The 45 mile wide caldera would unleash the power of molten rock trapped 125 miles under the surface. Almost twelve million years ago the hot spot, now centered on Yellowstone, was in southern Idaho. The supervolcano blew and left a covering of ash about ten feet deep as far away as eastern Nebraska. Most geologists agreed that this sort of cataclysmic eruption was one of the worst things that could happen to life on Earth. Fortunately, it only happens about every six hundred thousand years or so. Sheila knew that it has been about six hundred and thirty thousand years since the last eruption and that this seismic activity was not at all a good sign.

II

"That's the last of it," the doctor said grimly. Carmen Fletcher watched the patient's horror stricken face. The woman had the beginnings of an infection that would soon sweep throughout her body if left unchecked by penicillin, and she had just witnessed the doctor administer the last of the antibiotic.

"What does this mean?" she asked them both.

"It means," said the doctor, "that you're in for a pretty rough time. You're going to have to be strong."

Carmen didn't think the woman was looking particularly strong at that moment. "Stan," Carmen advocated, "we've got to get antibiotics from *some-where.*"

Stan nodded in assent. "Sure we do. Have you got any ideas where we're supposed to find some? Carmen, you know as well as I do that everyone within a day's drive of here is hoarding their supplies of *all* medications. They see what we're dealing with here and are predicting they'll have to deal with it too. I can't squeeze any more medicine out of thin air!"

She thought for a moment. "Alright," she began, thinking as she spoke. "Alright. Here's what we'll do. I've got a classmate who's a D.O. down in Denver. He's got a General Practice set up. I can drive down there and fill my car with Penicillin, Amoxicillin, whatever. With luck I can be back here in 24 hours. Think we can hold out that long?"

"Think we have another choice?" replied Stan.

I'll drive straight through," she said, looking directly at the patient. "24 hours round trip. Count on it!" and she trotted out to the parking lot. Though her Suburban had only been parked outside for three or four hours, the falling ash had accumulated on it again. She brushed the inches of it off like she would a winter snowfall. The choking dust blew around her in the Wyoming wind, getting in her eyes, ears and nose. Coughing and spluttering, she climbed into the relative comfort of her vehicle and started it. She drove through ash drifts that had been piling up all around town. Everywhere there was an eddy — spaces between buildings, ends of fence lines, around benches on the street — ash was collecting and drifting like snow. Already the state crews were using the snowplows to try to keep the highways clear but the ash was getting into the big trucks' works and stranding them next to the vehicles they were trying to help.

She said a silent prayer that her own SUV would be able to make it through the worst of it all the way to Denver. There was another complication weighing on here mind: The doctor in Denver was a former classmate of hers. They had been lovers in first year med school and had suffered an ugly breakup. She hadn't seen him in more than eight years and hadn't spoken to him in longer than that. As she drove up the onramp onto I-25 southbound she hoped that the world situation would be more important than their shared past.

Karl Roscoe

"Nice digs," said Dennis Schweigert, looking around the general's office. Dark wood and lush carpeting accented the huge space. The general's desk took up a substantial portion of acreage at the far end. It was flanked on either side by tall, deep bookshelves filled with a career's worth of trinkets and mementoes.

"It'll do," replied General William Grabowski, settled deeply into a plush leather chair at the head of a long conference table. "You sure you don't want something to eat or drink?"

"I'm fine. Thanks for putting me up last night, by the way," he said gratefully. "Really general, if you want to do something for me you can give me a helicopter to take to Sandpoint. My family is probably wondering what's taking me so long and I do need to get home."

The general sighed. "Son," he said, "your family is gone. Sandpoint is gone. ALL of northern Idaho is gone." He stood up and motioned for Dennis to join him. "Come over here. I want you to look at these." Slowly, reluctantly, Schweigert shuffled over to stand beside General Grabowski. "We can't get satellite photos of the region. The ash and debris have pierced the atmosphere up to 75,000 feet. It has created a cloud we won't be able to penetrate for weeks. But we do have radar and infrared." He indicated the maps spread out on the conference table in front of them. "These are the latest shots from Falcon Air Force Base."

Schweigert looked at the images. Someone had superimposed dotted lines on them depicting state and country boundaries. Something that appeared to be a ring of mountains surrounded one section of the picture. It was, according to Grabowski, a massive circular radar return, almost fifty miles in diameter. It engulfed the red outline marked 'Calgary.' Radiating outward to almost 100 miles were spokes of dust and debris. It looked like a gigantic wagon wheel. Where highways 2 and 95 should have clearly showed up on the radar, where Lake Pend Oreille and Priest Lake should have clearly reflected radar images, there was only the smooth of almost four feet of ash and ejecta, like a blizzard had blanketed the area.

A thick red band stretched around the circle, as far as Missoula and extending to the south of Lewiston. "That's the kill zone, son," said the general gently. "Nothing and nobody inside that zone survived. I'm sorry." It very clearly included the town of Sandpoint and the family he had left there.

Schweigert slumped into the seat next to the general. He lurched forward, cradling his head in his arms on the tabletop and began to sob. General Grabowski reached over and placed his arm clumsily around the broken man. He appeared self conscious and awkward as he tried to comfort him.

This was the scene presented to the President of the United States and his aide Mr. Palmer upon their arrival at Fort Carson.

Karl Roscoe

"What do you mean he's not here anymore?" Carmen Fletcher was frantic.

"He moved his practice down to the Springs about a year and a half ago," said the tired-looking receptionist. "Now if you'll excuse me, it is very late and I would like to go home."

"No!" pleaded a disbelieving Carmen. "You don't understand!"

"Sweetie, I understand perfectly. You want antibiotics. I don't authorize their transfer and the people who do have gone home already. Your friend has moved out of town. You want the meds? Drive to the Springs: He's working the rich people at the south end. Somewhere in the Broadmoor. Now excuse me and good night." While she spoke she walked toward Carmen, forcing her to walk backwards and out the door. Carmen found herself standing outside without the words she needed to stop this woman from making a terrible mistake. As the woman said "good night," she closed the door and locked it. With a plastic smile and a small wave she turned off the lights and headed for the back door.

An incredulous Carmen stood out in the lightly falling ash under a sky that was much darker than it should have been at 5:30 on a spring afternoon. Mark was down in Colorado Springs—more driving! Already she was six hours behind her self-imposed schedule and now she'd have to drive even further out of her way. Then she'd have to convince him to give her the medications. Then she'd have to drive back to Casper. There was no question she'd have to sleep at some point; already she was feeling more of the effects of lack of sleep over the past 22 or 23 hours. For now all she could do was press onward to his office and hope that someone would be there for her to talk to. She dragged her exhausted self to her Suburban, started the engine and, sighing deeply, began driving further south.

J effrey, how many times do I have to tell you, I don't want to do any God-damned USO shows!"

"Honey, it's not a show. It's a tour. You'll be touring a couple of bases in the area. One of them is even on the inside of a mountain!" He was trying to sound enthusiastic but it was coming off as irate.

"First of all, you know I don't tour," she snapped, "and second: Who the hell lives on the inside of a mountain?"

"Baby, listen to me." Unfortunately having to explain almost everything at its most base level was part of representing Ms. Alexis Coffey. Stifling the deep breath he usually took before launching into his explanation, Jeff Cole spoke as slowly and clearly as he could. "You will be joining a group of people who are going inside the mountain to look at a military base inside. They built this base during the cold war to withstand a nuclear blast. Now they use it for...well they use it for *something*. I don't know what the hell it is. Anyway it is a big deal. You'll enjoy it. Trust me." He struggled to keep the smile in his voice when he finished.

"How am I supposed to enjoy some military thing? This is so stupid!"

"OK sugar, here's the deal. People have to wait for more than a year to get a spot on this tour. I had to call in a lot of cards to get you in. Some bigwigs said it was OK but only if you do a little meet and greet with them. Please, baby, you'll have almost as much fun as you're having at that hotel."

"Yeah, about the hotel Jeffrey...."

"Now, you can't possibly tell me you don't like it?!"

"Well the lake is nice, except for the ducks or whatever those disgusting beasts shitting all over the sidewalks are. And the food is fine. There's all these geeky golfers roaming around and old ladies with tennis rackets."

"So what's not to like, Alex?" He began signaling towards his secretary indicating that he needed to get off this call.

"I don't like being *here*, Jeffrey. I want to be back *there*! I mean, what if I miss something? What if somebody throws a 'must' party and I'm stuck in this nowhere stupid town?"

"Baby, go on the tour tomorrow. Be nice to the old men. Maybe they can pull some strings and get you a helicopter ride or something. Ever think of that?"

"OK," she pouted, "but I won't like it!"

Sheila Sokolowski was driving out to inspect yet another hot spot when her radio crackled to life.

"Sheila, it's Peter. Can you read?"

She was navigating around a particularly difficult stretch of what used to be road when he called. Without taking her eyes off the track in front of her, she reached for the walkie-talkie on the seat beside her and depressed the microphone button. "Yeah, Pete, I've got you loud and clear. You can sure pick some lousy times to interrupt me."

"Sheila, you need to listen." His voice was urgent. "We're getting beta wave activity like crazy out of the whole park. Rock is fracturing everywhere. I think this may be it."

She abruptly stopped the pickup truck where it was and sat motionless behind the wheel. Slowly she raised the radio to her mouth and said "Have you called Washington?"

He answered promptly. "Still trying to raise them. Everyone is so busy with the meteor they don't have time for the Geological Survey folks. At least not us out here."

"OK Peter. Keep trying. If that doesn't work try the media outlets. Anything you can think of to get the word out. Perhaps a bit of hysteria will get their attention." She was thoughtful for a moment and then spoke again. "Any idea how long?"

"We're guessing it'll happen before you get back...couple hours tops." There was a long pause. "It's been great working with you, Sheila." His voice was choked with emotion.

"You too, Peter. Go home to your family." She reached down and almost absent-mindedly turned off the power to the radio. Then she got out of the truck and moved to the front end. Climbing on the hood, she sat back against the windshield and considered the blackened sky. She pulled her jacket around her to ward off the chill, pondered how much she had valued her time in this most special of places on earth and waited for the inevitable explosion.

Between six hundred and thirty and six hundred and fifty thousand years ago, Yellowstone volcano blew up. Considering that modern man is only about 120,000 years old, no human being has ever seen anything so powerful, so violent, so cataclysmic. The blast lifted about 2500 times the material of the Mount St. Helens eruption into the atmosphere. The detonation itself flattened, sterilized and incinerated hundreds of miles around the volcano's crater. Ash, magma and gas were ejected in all directions and covered the ground thousands of miles away. Los Angeles was covered in ash. Northern Mexico was covered. Iowa and Minnesota and Manitoba, Saskatchewan and Alberta were all buried under inches of ash. Virtually all of North America west of the Mississippi river was blanketed with cinder more than ten feet deep in places.

Animals that survived the initial destruction were subjected to wandering, parched, through this silica-rich dust. They were literally slicing their lungs and drowning from the fluids as they were forced to breathe it in. There was no solace at lakes and rivers. The ash created a sludge that was impossible to drink. They all dropped dead of starvation, suffocation and thirst.

The eruption lifted enough material into the atmosphere to dim the light of the sun for months. Within 72 hours, the ash cloud covered the earth. Without the warming influence of the sun, global temperatures dropped by 70 degrees Fahrenheit in a matter of days. Unable to photosynthesize, plants were killed in droves. Animals, dependant on those plants, began to starve. Once thought to be a refuge, the oceans were equally affected. Carbon dioxide levels rose and the ocean absorbed the increase. This effectively increased the acidity of the water and dissolved the shells of the zooplankton. Phytoplankton were unable to reproduce or even live. Without these beings to form the base of the food chain, life in the oceans began to falter.

After a few months the ash fall let up and the sun began shining through. The planet was able to warm up fairly rapidly but the worst was far from over. Sulfides and methane and other greenhouse gasses released during the eruption hung high in the atmosphere. Rather than releasing the sun's reflected heat from the surface of the Earth, they trapped it, much like a blanket. So the planet went from a prolonged freeze cycle to an extended runaway heat cycle.

As if that wasn't enough, the sulfur particles in the atmosphere formed the basis for clouds. These clouds circled the globe dropping noxious acid rain, poisoning the natural water supplies and making it further impossible for life to regain any kind of toehold on the wrecked planet. Some speculate it took hundreds of thousands of years for what we would consider normal life to return to the earth.

Karl Roscoe

Agustin Sanchez was getting nervous. The military guard had held up his truck for more than half an hour and was showing no sign of allowing him to continue. He had made excellent time on his new route and was planning on being home tomorrow morning. Now, at the south end of Colorado Springs, he had been hindered by a military check point and his cargo was being scrutinized. Still a full eight hours away at just above the speed limit, this delay was proving unbearable. He had been on the cell phone with his wife all day. She was as anxious as he was. Louisa had never been entirely comfortable in the United States and felt best when he was home to provide an anchor for the family.

The military policeman approached his truck. "We're gonna need you to pull up to that holding area over there," he said pointing up the road.

"Officer," said Agustin, "can't you please let me continue on? I need to drop this load in Salt Lake for the customer and I'd like to get back to my family as quickly as possible."

"First of all, it's Private," he drawled. "I am *definitely* not an officer. Secondly, we'll get you rolling along as soon as we offload those generators. You'll see your family soon enough."

"Wait," said Agustin, desperation beginning to rise in his voice. "I am responsible for these generators. This is my load! You can't just take them off my truck! That's stealing!"

"OK," said the soldier matter-of-factly, "Here's how this works: The U.S. Army has declared eminent domain over all power production devices. Because of the national emergency, we're in the power business now. I suggest you pull your truck over to the staging area and wait for further instructions." He was looking Agustin square in the eye as he said this. There was no mistaking the undertone of threat coming from the man. Grudgingly, Agustin did as he was told.

He had had difficult trips before, mostly due to hazardous loads or impossible customers, but this time it was different. There was something really frightening happening in the world and he was away from the people he cared about most; the people who needed him the most right now.

For the first time in his professional life he began to see his chosen trade as an enemy. It was not a good feeling.

Another soldier guided him into a growing line of trucks carrying a number of different loads. They were all to report to the Fort Carson distribution point for further evaluation. The convoy of vehicles, led by a humvee with a flashing blue light, drove slowly through the town of Colorado Springs. Agustin fretted as he drove slowly along. A few stray onlookers stared and pointed at the convoy but most just hurried along through the gray gloom, busy on their own errands. He dialed his wife to deliver yet another bulletin from the trip from hell. As expected, she was not happy. She was a strong-minded woman. When she wanted something from him, she made her wishes clear in an unequivocal fashion. He told her he would do everything he could to be home the next day.

Karl Roscoe

Hiroki Nagamachi was again on the phone to his friend Ed Beidelmann. "We're seeing it everywhere, Ed," Hiroki exclaimed passionately. "Richter fours, tremors, temblors, pre-volcanic beta wave indicators...I'm telling you, we've never seen so much activity. It seems to be centered everywhere!"

"OK Hiroki, slow down a bit. We're seeing some of it too, in isolated patches. Yellowstone is what has me most concerned right now."

"Yes," said Hiroki, "Yellowstone is velly active now." Beidelmann winced. When Hiroki got excited he lost his grip on his otherwise textbook perfect English and dropped his r's in favor of the easier to say l's. "*Very* active," he corrected himself. "Ed, I'm getting pretty scared over here. It appears that the meteor has loosened up something critical in the crust and things are just starting to let go. Not that I'd be the one to call it but we appear to be at the beginning of a major tectonic plate shift. There's more going on seismically right now than we have volcanologists and geologists to study.

More bad news was the last thing that Beidelmann had wanted to hear. The President had insisted on daily updates and was getting more nervous with the information coming in. "Alright, spell this out for me. **Where** exactly are we talking about, Hiroki?"

"The entire Pacific rim. South America, north to Alaska and the Aleutians, down the Kurile trench, the Japan and Ryukyu trenches southward to Indonesia and the Tonga trench. Ed, I've never seen or read anything like this. We're talking Armageddon here."

"My God," breathed Beidelmann. "We've been so focused on Yellowstone and Seattle we forgot to monitor the rest of the world. Hiroki, do you have a place to go?"

"Ed," said his friend, thousands of miles distant, "no-one does."

Carmen Fletcher had finally found her former lover. He was established in a comfortable office in southern Colorado Springs tending to the skinned knees and coughs and colds of Colorado Springs' elite. Immediately she filled him in on everything she would need. Despite her exhausted state and frenzy to communicate, she was able to convey everything. He actually surprised her and even one-upped her request. He made a few phone calls and within an hour a driver was northbound with a semi-truck full of all kinds of medications for her hospital. While he was on the phone she stole a few glances at him. He was taller than she remembered. Every bit as handsome, though. And it seemed that he'd been working out—his body was lean and muscular. It was easy to see why she'd fallen for him so long ago.

"And you," he smiled after hanging up from the last call, "will spend the rest of the evening with me. You look like you could use a glass of wine and about 48 hours of sleep."

She almost cried on the spot. A glass of wine! How long had it been since she'd been able to enjoy such a simple pleasure?

"There is one catch," he said. "I need to make a quick stop out at Cheyenne Mountain. One of my clients needs a checkup and doesn't really trust the military medical system. Sort of a side deal, you know," he winked at her.

Now she was reminded why they'd broken up. Despite his obvious physical attractiveness, Mark was an ethical tar pit. When they were in med school he'd expressed the intention to do something for mankind with his degree. The way he treated people—including her—belied that intention and exposed the true man behind the smile. She found herself halfway between revulsion toward his dealsmanship and gratitude for the generous donation of medications. Despite her own best judgment, she agreed to go on the house call.

On the drive over to the military base he outlined his past few years to catch her up. He said he'd tried to go the humanitarian route (which she doubted seriously) but very quickly discovered that humanitarian cases don't cover the bills. After running into an old friend who was currently living in the south end of Colorado Springs, he discovered the little goldmine. As far as the work went, there was nothing more than the occasional broken arm or heart attack. He started by opening an office there for two days a week. Very quickly it showed how profitable it could be and, after about a year of increasing success in the area, he made the decision to pack up his practice altogether and move southward.

Since then his patient list had grown astronomically and now included several heavy hitters—including the general they were now on their way to see. The way he'd relayed the story it all sounded very rational and reasonable but Carmen could clearly see that this was not the old Mark Zorbas that she'd been crazy about in school. There was an unidentifiable sheen on his personality, like a fine mist of oil, slicking up every point he tried to make. She felt that she wanted to wash her hands after having a conversation with him. And just like she'd felt immediately after the breakup, she was uncomfortable merely being in his presence.

Fortunately, the drive didn't take very much longer. They were at the base of a long, winding road that led up the side of a mountain. Cheyenne Mountain, Mark had called it. He said that they had dug a military base out of living rock back in the 60's. At least she'd have something to occupy her thoughts other than the dubious character sitting beside her. At the top of the road they parked the car and boarded a waiting trolley. It took them down a long tunnel where they were ushered in past a monstrous bank-vault-looking door and into the base. A short walk through a couple of buildings led them to their destination.

About twenty minutes later, Mark finished up his examination and was just coming out of the general's private office. "Mac," he said, "you've gotta layoff the fatty foods. We're definitely going to see a spike in your blood cholesterol and that'll seal it for you."

"Okay, Doc," said the officer, shaking his hand. "I'll tell the galley hands to see if they can't come up with something appetizing that won't kill me!"

Carmen stood up to join the two when there was a commotion in the hallway. An airman burst through the door and called out "General! The world is blowing up!"

I t was past lunchtime and Alexis Coffey was being bustled down some corridor in a massive herd of military uniforms. She had started her goodwill tour of the local area military bases at Fort Carson. Seconds before she had been looking down at the bald pate of some presumably important person, seeing the distorted reflection of herself. The next thing she knew, people were shouting about destruction and fires and magma and God knows what else. So she allowed herself to be carried along in this river of humanity, rushed onto a bus and transported to a place everyone was calling 'The Mountain.'

She noticed immediately that the earlier icky, gray sky had turned to a threatening black, as if a massive thunderhead had moved in. The ash fall which, up until now had been like a light snow drifting from the sky, had become a hideous blizzard. It was pelting straight down from the sky in waves. The inconsistent drone of sandy pellets made a buzzing sound on the top of their bus. It almost sounded as if wave after wave of angry bees was attacking the vehicle. Suddenly there was a sharp BANG and the occupants looked up to see a huge dent in the ceiling. Apparently there were rocks mixed in with the rest of this storm.

'Why do you people even *live* here?!" she shouted at the person sitting next to her. "This place sucks!"

The person in question looked at her disbelievingly and ducked toward the seat in front, hoping for more cover. The bus was able to make it to the entrance of Cheyenne Mountain without stalling. It parked just outside the tunnel entrance where a host of cars had already been abandoned. Alexis was pushed off the bus by the frightened horde and swept into the confines of the military complex. One guard stood his post next to the tunnel entrance and made no attempt to stop the flood of people coming through. Alexis found herself in a long tunnel surrounded by throngs of people all shouting at one another. Down, down they went till they came to an entryway with massive steel vault-like doors. Just before she entered she saw a woman with several small children off to one side. The children clutched at their mother while she crouched there, weeping.

Leah Sandon kissed her husband goodbye and collected the children. Their lunch together had been another gift from God and she was thankful. She reminded the children what a good man Caleb was and that they all had God's favor. Then, followed by her small brood, she got aboard the trolley which would carry them through the tunnel and drop them at the parking lot. Walking from the edge of the fence around and through the parked vehicles to their minivan, she looked to the sky to praise God in His goodness and beheld a terrible spectacle. To the north the sky grew black; rising up from the earth like a curtain and spreading quickly in all directions. Then came the noise: A deafening howling roar, followed by a pelting from millions of grains of grit. She looked over her left shoulder to be sure that Ruth had baby

Rebecca covered up when she heard a dull thud.

Ruth's eyes grew saucer-round and she dropped the baby in her car seat to scream in horror. She pointed to Leah's right. Fear pulsing hard in her chest, Leah spun in the opposite direction to see her eldest son Jacob kneeling by the side of his brother. Joshua, the beautiful eight-year-old, had had his head crushed by a piece of stone flying from the sky. The immense dent in his skull faced upward as he lay motionless between the cars. Blood ebbed slowly from the wound and pooled on the ground around his head like a grisly halo. There was no mistaking that he was dead.

Now Leah screamed in turn and rushed to his side. All the children were screaming and sobbing. Jacob was pulling on Joshua's arm yelling "Come on! Get up!" Dropping to her knees, Leah pulled his lifeless body to her breast and sobbed hysterically. Through all the noise and confusion Leah heard a small voice. "Momma! **Momma!**" She looked up and Ruth was pointing again. Rocks were falling from the sky and striking the cars all around them. "Momma, it's not safe! Where should we go?"

Torn between a son she could not save and four other children she could, she retched out an agonized scream. She gently laid Joshua back down on the asphalt, stood and, as calmly as she could manage, lined the children in front of her. "Back inside, kids. NOW. We have to find your father." Staggering, sobbing, dodging bits of falling rock and hopelessly looking back over her shoulder at her son's small body, they made their way back to the main entrance of the tunnel. Cars began screeching up along the fence. Four guards posted outside the tunnel's entrance unshouldered their M-16's and began roughly shoving people back out into the falling debris. They recognized the family that had just left and allowed them inside. After hustling her family almost a quarter of a mile underground, Leah finally moved off to one side near the entry gate by the blast doors and gathered her children protectively around her.

"I'll go find Dad," volunteered Jacob, and disappeared into the depths of the mountain.

Karl Roscoe

Viktor Kasparof was gazing vacantly out the window when he saw a large section of the earth spew upward and outward. In heavily accented English he called out to the American and Italian astronauts, "Hey, where are we?"

Antonio DiGiammo looked up from the experiment he was working on. A glance at the clock told him what he needed to know. "North America, why?" "Come look at this, quickly." DiGiammo floated over to join Kasparof at the window. A pinpoint of red glow emanated from the crust of the Earth with a fountain of black material gushing skyward. The blackness spread as rapidly outward as it did upward. "Holy shit!" he exclaimed, adopting the American phrase easily. "What's going on down there?"

Phillip Narita, the International Space Station's second in command, came from another module. "What's all the noise about?" he said.

"Look here," said Kasparof, his voice grim.

Narita floated over to share the viewing pod. "Not again," he breathed. The explosion had diffused enough to begin to blend in with the ashen remains of the meteor strike but there was clearly a darkened area spreading further and further outward. Already the circle of darkness extended from its western Wyoming center to Reno, Nevada. Northward it passed the northern border of the U.S. and it pushed as far south as New Mexico. To the east it had already reached eastern South Dakota. "What the Christ is happening to our planet?" he whispered.

Kasparof, remembering himself as station commander, was already on the radio. "Houston, is Unity here. How copy?" There was a too long silence, then he tried again. "Houston, is Unity Station. Respond please."

Another long pause before the radio crackled to life. "Unity, we have you loud and clear. Guys, we know why you're calling and the truth is we don't really know what is happening. Perhaps you can help us shed a little light on it."

Kasparof handed the microphone over to Narita. "OK, Houston. Narita here. Looks like a plume originating in the west—Wyoming or Montana from the looks of it. Large explosion. A very large dark cloud erupting from the center and spreading rapidly."

The Italian poked Narita's shoulder. 'Tell them about

the red glow in the center."

Narita keyed the mic again. "Ahh, Houston, it seems that there was red in the center." He released the transmission key and queried DiGiammo, "What red?"

DiGiammo took the microphone away from Narita and spoke. "DiGiammo here now, Houston. At the core of the plume there was a red center. Did not last very long before it was covered by fallout."

Houston responded, "Did you see another meteor?"

DiGiammo looked at Kasparof who shook his head vigorously. "Negative, negative. Just the explosion."

There was another long silence. "OK gentlemen, we still don't seem to have any idea what it is. At this time command wants you to get back to work and we'll keep you apprised of the situation. How copy?"

DiGiammo handed the microphone once more to the Kasparof. "Copy," he said curtly. "You realize difficulty of work in this situation...."

"Affirmative," came the flat reply from Houston. "Just do the best you can, Unity."

Karl Roscoe

A n SUV with darkly tinted windows wound its way slowly through the knot of cars on the road to Cheyenne Mountain. More than once it pulled off the road and drove up the yucca strewn meadows stretching out to either side. They made better time off the road than on but were continuously forced back to the pavement by stands of scrub oak blocking the way. Eventually they got to the parking lot at the top and the tunnel outlet. There were throngs of yelling people attempting to get past the armed security policemen defending the entrance. All four car doors opened at once and three big men in dark suits and sunglasses began pushing a path into and through the crowd. Behind them marched the President of the United States, his aide Mr. Palmer, General Grabowski and his guest Dennis Schweigert.

At the far end of the crowd a secret service agent stepped in front of the guards and told them to stand aside.

"Buddy, I don't know who you are but I can tell you that I'm not moving even if the President of the United States himself tells me to!" replied the young military policeman, brandishing his weapon.

"Not even if I make it a direct order?" said the President, pushing out of the crowd behind his agents.

The M.P.'s jaw dropped and he stared incredulously. Recovering quickly, the soldier immediately snapped to attention with his gun pointed downward. "Of course, sir," he said, his eyes wide with fear. "Yes, Mr. President, go right on through!" His comrades gaped in open amazement at seeing the President right there, unannounced. People in the crowd began shouting "We want answers!"…"What's happening to us?"…and "Save us Mr. President!" The guards gave way and the President with his entourage walked into the tunnel. The crowd began pressing against the guards again. They gave one last attempt at holding the people back before relenting. One MP broke and ran into the tunnel creating a void for the crowd. Immediately people rushed forward to follow the Presidential party. Two dropped their weapons where they stood and ran out into the gathering gloom of the day, racing on foot, presumably, to their homes below. The final guard slung his shoulder strap around the back of his neck and rested his arms on the top of the weapon. He watched idly as hundreds people pushed into the confines of one of the most secret places on earth.

Down into the tunnel marched the assemblage with the President at the lead. At the security station at the entrance to the base, another Security Policeman had the opportunity to be shocked by seeing the President. He allowed the main detail through. The others he tried to stop at the entrance by closing the vault door. His effort was hopeless. The crowd of people forced their bodies through the closing space. Eventually the mob was able to push the vault door back on its immense hinges. The guard called for backup but hundreds of civilians were now pouring into the Cheyenne Mountain complex.

Once past the mountain's sentry gate, General Grabowski took the lead and guided the group toward the nerve center of the subterranean base. Badges were flashed and workers allowed the group to get deeper and deeper into the complex. Finally, just outside the Combat Ops Center, they were stopped by a young sergeant who had no intention of letting them go further. "I'm sorry, sir," she said. "You certainly *look* like the President but my orders are that no-one gets through here. No-one."

A very reasonable-sounding General Grabowski said "Sergeant, a single call and all this can be cleared up. May I please use your phone?"

She looked at him uncertainly and then pushed the telephone across the desk. The two Security Police guards behind her planted their feet firmly on the floor, reiterating their commitment to their orders.

"General McIntyre — do you have his number?"

She consulted a list on her desk and said "Dial 3-4640."

The general dialed the phone and waited for a moment "Sharon? Hi, it's Bill Grabowski. Is Mac in?" Another moment and then, "Yes, it's quite important actually. I have the President of the United States with me and he wants to speak with the general." There was a noise of someone saying a few things quite loudly on the other end of the phone and General Grabowski smiled. "Yes, he arrived somewhat unexpectedly. He came to see another guest I have out here with me. May we come in?" He nodded slowly and said "Alright, here she is." Handing the phone over to the gatekeeper he said "Excellent work, Sergeant. Your country can be proud of you." The Sergeant took the phone a little uncertainly. "I believe Sharon will provide you with the necessary clearance."

The woman put the receiver to her ear, feeling both ashamed and proud at the same time. After a moment's talking she hung up and said, "You are all cleared to pass." They began walking into the secure zone when she stood and said "Mr. President..." He turned toward her and she offered a precise, formal salute. "It's an honor, sir." The President returned the salute and then offered his hand to shake. "It is me who has the honor of working with professionals like you, Sergeant...Harris," he said, reading her nametag. She flushed and beamed and the group continued on.

This day had begun like any other. The people of Seattle went about their business in the dull gray mist, although they looked more frequently at the hulking shadow of Mount Rainier forty miles to the south and east. They had been told to expect bad things from their dangerous neighbor. Many experts were warning of cataclysm and recommended getting north or south as far and as quickly as possible. Some heeded the call, getting on the occasional airplane that was brave (or foolish) enough to fly through the thick remains of the meteor fallout. Others packed their cars and headed toward California or Canada, away from the menacing giant in their backyard. But most stayed on and hoped for the best. After all, hadn't the mountains always been here? Hadn't they heard the rumbling and threats of volcanic eruption before? And even though St. Helens burped in such a dramatic fashion back in '80, didn't that turn out to be nothing more than a minor inconvenience for the people unfortunate enough to live just downwind?

So it was that, despite the warnings of Ed Beidelmann and others, they were caught virtually completely unprepared when Rainier finally burst under the mounting pressure of the magma below. It was a truly spectacular sight. In a matter of seconds, the millions of tons of rock, earth, snow and ice that made up the top two-thirds of the fourteen-thousand foot peak were retched upwards. The debris cloud topped thirty-thousand feet in less than five seconds. The magma melted the ice and snow instantly and it mixed with the rock, ash and soil. The result was a pyroclastic river of sludge, flowing rapidly downward and seeking the path of least resistance. Since the blast favored the north side of the mountain, the flow concentrated in the lush valleys that led directly toward Tacoma, the SeaTac Airport and, ultimately, Seattle itself.

The city fathers had long since prepared for this eventuality. In fact, they had the file readily available. Upon opening it they were dismayed to discover that the authors of the study had never planned for a worst-case scenario and, even more distressingly, had planned heavily on using the SeaTac Airport, Boeing Field and McChord Air Force Base as evacuation centers. No-one had ever considered that aircraft would be useless. The city officials transitioned immediately from a strong group of leaders into a pack of terrified children when they discovered that there would be no organized escape. Rather than alerting the public to this gross oversight, the city officials adopted a wait-and-hope posture. It was, they conceded, too late now to create a new strategy.

The blast took a few seconds to traverse the forty-something miles from Rainier to downtown Seattle. The first thing that people noticed was the pressure wave spreading outward, followed by the ghastly noise of the earth exploding. Those who were looking could see the explosion long before they could hear it — an eerie few seconds of watching the world fly apart before any other sensations could verify what their eyes were recording. Those who weren't looking at the peak instantly snapped their heads to the south to confirm what they already expected to see. A massive dark pillar rose into the gray gloom, casting further shadow on the doomed city. Its frantic occupants jumped into whatever vehicles were available and began to search for an escape. Violent fights broke out. People were pushed down into the streets while others attempted to steal their keys and cars. It simply didn't matter.

Traveling at over 200 miles per hour, the flow took less than 15 minutes to reach downtown Seattle and Puget Sound. It swept over people, trees, buildings and anything else in its way as easily as a tidal wave would wipe out a sand castle on the beach. Some were even caught unawares in their homes; coffee cups in hand, earphones playing their favorite tunes while they diddled at their computer keyboards. Following the path of countless other eruptions, the flow made its relentless way to the ocean. The valleys of Washington were once again flooded in the rich lava that would one day produce another rainforest full of new and different life.

Caleb Sandon's face was a stone mask as he walked very quickly through the hallways inside the mountain. The son did his best to keep up with his silent father, occasionally having to break into a trot just to keep him in sight. After winding through the throng of civilians being held in check by a security detail, Caleb stepped out into the tunnel where saw his wife crouched by the near wall with their daughter and the twin babies sitting close by. Her face was reddened, streaks of dirt tracking downward over her cheeks; her eyes swollen and ugly. Caleb knelt by her side and placed a protective arm around her shoulders. Leah looked into her husband's gaze and burst into another racking round of sobs. The children watched their parents in horrified silence.

At last Leah's crying subsided and she haltingly told Caleb the heart wrenching details of the death of their son.

"Can you take me to the boy?" he asked.

She shook her head violently. "I won't look at him again like that, Caleb. I can't."

Caleb turned to his eldest son. "Jacob, can you take me to him?"

Jacob gulped and nodded his head slowly. He had no desire whatsoever to see his brother's lifeless body again, but his father, the anchor of the family, his protector and hero, had asked him to do something and he was helpless to deny that wish. "Come on, Dad," he said with a wavering voice barely above a whisper. "He's in the parking lot."

As if he had all the weight of the world on his shoulders, Jacob made his way back up the tunnel to the entrance of the mountain. Outside the larger rocks and pebbles had finished falling, replaced by ash and fine dust filtering downward. Mustering all the courage his mind and body could, the ten-year-old led his father through the parking lot. The abandoned cars had all been damaged by the fallout. Some had their roofs or hoods collapsed by the larger stones. Others were dented like demolition derby contenders. None had an unbroken windshield. The falling debris had begun piling up like snowdrifts everywhere. Dust and ash mounded against car tires where the breeze was unable to push through. Theirs were the only footprints in the parking lot.

Jacob led Caleb through the maze of cars to where his brother's body lay under a blanket of gray silt. He was unprepared to hear his father's sharp intake of breath—the choking back of involuntary sobs. Now the eldest son was invisible as his father gave in to the grief for his lost boy. Falling hard to his knees beside the Joshua's dust covered body, he reached out to gather him into his arms. The boy's head lolled to the left to reveal the large depression where the rock had crushed his skull. Clotting blood mixed with dust and ash to form an ugly, congealed mass. As his father lifted Joshua's body, his head rolled over and back, bouncing once on the ground with a sickening thud. Jacob turned away, eyes burning with tears. He couldn't stand to watch.

With no more control left, Caleb cried out to the heavens. "Why, my Lord? Why have you chosen my son?" Cradling the boy's body and rocking back and forth he sobbed. "Dear God, you are all powerful. Return him to us as you did with Lazarus. In Jesus' name I ask you, Lord!" He bowed his head over his son's corpse, hugging him close. "Please, dear Lord, trade my life for his. In your son's holy name, I ask this of you."

For a long time the father embraced the son who would not come back to life. The other, with his back turned to the scene, wondered at the change in Caleb. Always in command, always the leader, always the cornerstone. Now he was reduced to a tearful wreck. Jacob was uncomfortable witnessing this kind of weakness and he didn't know how to deal with it. So he stood quietly and took a few steps away, waiting for his father to finish grieving.

Finally, lifting Joshua in his arms, Caleb stood and began walking through the eerily swirling gray dust back to mountain's entrance. Jacob followed, this time having no difficulty keeping up. They were stopped at the entrance of the tunnel by a new detail of police who were now guarding the access way.

"I'm sorry, sir, but you can't bring him in here. General's orders." He said the words as gently as he could but his demeanor left no doubt that he would back up the words with whatever action became necessary.

Caleb looked at the guard, moonfaced; wordlessly pleading.

"I'm very sorry, sir," the Security Policeman said again. "You'll have to leave him here"

Jacob waited impatiently for the father he knew to take command. To order the sergeant to step aside; that an officer was about to carry his son past their feeble post. But that didn't happen. He watched his father crumple slowly into a pile of defeat. Whimpering and crying softly, Caleb stroked his son's lifeless face. Unable to participate in his father's breakdown any longer, Jacob walked between the guards to rejoin his mother and other siblings.

"So you're saying this thing is going to blow us all up?"

"No, General," Dennis patiently explained. "We all tend to place things within a frame of reference we can best understand." He waved a hand around the office, indicating the flag, the medals, the mementos on the shelves. "This is not a military thing. This is physics, geology, meteorology: Science. Not politics."

"Fine," interrupted General Grabowski. "Explain the science again."

It was evening. The official party had gathered in General McIntyre's conference room to hear the briefing the President had been requesting for days. Inside the mountain were the thousand or so military and civilian employees plus the four hundred some-odd civilians who had forced their way in. These people were being kept isolated from the military facility in several rooms.

"OK," began Dennis slowly, "we all know about the asteroid. Now here's the really bad part: It managed to hit one of the worst possible locations on the planet. General," he motioned to Grabowski, "picture the shock waves emanating off from an exploding Howitzer shell or a bomb. The waves go outward, expanding the destruction zone. What happened with the meteor is similar. These waves flowed outward, cracking the Earth's crust as they went. Look at this map." He gestured to a map of North America. "The energy of the asteroid was almost incalculable. Sure, that energy is dissipated as the waves radiate but they're still capable of an immense amount of damage. The plate shift off the west coast that created the tsunami is a prime example. Now let's start drawing our damage circles. As we know…" he faltered and winced as he pointed toward northern Idaho, "everything in this zone was obliterated. In fact, everything inside of *this* zone," indicating the next ring outward, "was wiped out, even though it wasn't directly impacted. Nothing was able to survive due to the heat and shockwaves. Now," he traced the third of the concentric circles, "there's still plenty of earth-cracking energy left in this wave." This was the circle approaching the Wyoming border. Passing his hand across the Yellowstone area he said, "If I am correct, we are currently experiencing the fallout of a massive, almost unimaginably powerful volcanic eruption."

"Wait a minute," said General McIntyre. "There's no volcano in that part of the country."

"I'm afraid there is, Mac," said the President. "In fact, Yellowstone is one of the largest volcanoes on the planet if my memory serves. Forty miles across, is that correct?" he asked Schweigert.

"Your people have briefed you well, Mr. President. Yes, Yellowstone caldera is about forty-five miles across."

"But my people also assured me that this caldera was stable—that we shouldn't be concerned in our lifetimes," countered the President.

"Under the circumstances existing when you were briefed, I'd say yes, sir. But, back to the map, these waves are cracking and shattering the crust as they radiate outward. Imagine one of your shells impacting on land 50 yards away from a frozen lake."

"Ice cubes," chuckled General Grabowski.

"Those ice cubes are what was holding the cap on one of the world's largest volcanoes," said Schweigert gravely. "And right now what we are witnessing is only the beginning of the horror."

The President snapped his head up. "What do you mean, 'the horror'?"

Dennis took a deep breath. "OK," he said, "none of this is going to be good." He began to pace and looked down at the floor, the table, anything but the faces of the men in the room. "Had the asteroid hit virtually any other place in the world, we would have what would equate to about one or two years of nuclear winter."

"But..." said General McIntyre.

"But it hit where it did and cracked the top off Yellowstone. Not only did the energy of the impact do that," he turned to the map again, "but the waves propagated outward and in *all* directions." He pointed at the northwest. "Rainier, Adams, St. Helens, Mt. Baker, Mt. Hood, Shasta...gentlemen, virtually the entire 'Ring of Fire' is at risk of destabilization."

General McIntyre leaned forward in his seat again. "So the whole world *is* going to blow up, then."

Dennis sighed again. "General, the crust all over the Earth is weakening. Its weakest points are called subduction zones—that's where one tectonic plate slides beneath another. There the molten goo that those plates float around on starts seeping out. From a planetary standpoint it's a little like getting a facelift. No blowing up involved. Unfortunately, at the scale of one human being, this facelift becomes catastrophic pretty quickly."

Ashen-faced, the President asked "Just what exactly are you saying, Mr. Schweigert?"

"Mr. President; gentlemen: What I am saying is...that we are currently facing the sixth great extinction on the planet Earth."

"Uh," said General Grabowski, "you're going to have to bring me up to speed. **Six** extinctions?"

Dennis sat down to join the men at the table. "Consider this," he said. "Billions of years ago, after the initial formation of Gondwana and Laurasia—those were super continents—there is evidence of a major climate change. This change is responsible for having killed off an immense number of creatures existing at the time. That's extinction number one: The Ordovician. Next came the Frasnian/late Devonian extinction. Since the majority of the Earth was, even more so than now, composed of water, this one wiped out corals and other water dwelling animals."

He was in the teaching mode now and began to warm to his subject. "Number three is sometimes called the 'Mother of all Extinctions.' It happened during the transition from the Paleozoic to the Mesozoic. Remember your 9th grade biology? Kingdom, phylum, class, order, family, genus, species, etc...? This one wiped out 57% of the *families* on Earth. Ninety-five percent of all marine life perished. Ninety-five percent, never to be seen on this planet again."

Dennis was hitting his stride. "Next came the Triassic and that was followed by the one we're all familiar with: The Cretaceous."

The President interjected. "Cretaceous is the one that killed the dinosaurs?"

"Yes sir. It left evidence of an asteroid's damage in the KT boundary layer. Famous and significant to us but to tell you the truth, it was pretty small as extinctions go. At least as compared to the Permian—the one that wiped out the families and almost all life in the ocean."

The President's aide, Mr. Palmer, spoke for the first time. "Do...do you think this will be as bad as those?"

Schweigert looked thoughtful. "Gentlemen, I've been predicting gloom and doom for a long time now. I've preached preparation and forethought but even I couldn't have foreseen destruction of this magnitude. All of the extinctions I've told you about are a direct result of climate change. Most of them directly due to volcanic activity. What we have happening to our world is beyond my own worst predictions. This event *will* kill virtually every form of life in our world. Perhaps a few plant and animal life forms may endure but, much above the level of bacteria...the odds are too remote to calculate."

The room was quiet for a long time. Then the President spoke. "How long do we have?"

"Weeks, probably. Months, possibly." He looked around the room and then asked McIntyre, "General, how long can we all survive in this mountain?"

McIntyre balked. "I'm afraid that's classified information, son."

"Oh, for God's sake, Mac! Classified from whom?" erupted General Grabowski. "We're trapped underground. What is there, a thousand, fifteen hundred of us? Tell the man how long we can live in here!"

McIntyre wrinkled his brow. "Independent water source, food supplies for a thousand.... I can probably augment from the outside for at least two or three weeks. I suppose with luck and care we could squeeze two years out down here."

Immediately General Grabowski said, "I'd like to get my family into the mountain."

"As would I," returned the President, "but it doesn't look like it's going to happen."

Grabowski fixed his gaze upon the President of the United States. This could not be possible! He was being told that his family would have to stay outside and perish. His scowl was met with an equally unyielding glare.

"I'm sorry Bill, but this is it." The President was grave and unwavering. "As of this moment, whoever is in the mountain stays in the mountain. No newcomers; no losses. I'm afraid that this little band has just become the best hope for human life on our planet."

Another strained silence while the two men stared each other down. Finally the spell was broken when Mr. Palmer cried, "You've *got* to be shitting me! You can't even be serious! Are you actually trying to tell me that every living thing that is not inside this mountain is going to freakin' die in the next two weeks?!"

Schweigert studied his hands clasped on the tabletop. He thought of his colleagues and students in Panama. He thought about an entire planet of life and all its diversity. "Yes," he replied. And that was all he could say.

Agustin Sanchez was pacing nervously around his tractor. The trailer had long since been removed and carted off to places unknown. Currently that was the least of his concerns. He was told that he could not leave the mountain according to the 'higher ups' and was cooling his heels waiting for 'their' approval.

The Army had escorted him through the south portal, past the main entrance and had him park near the mouth of the north portal. Once there they disconnected his load and hauled it off. He'd offered them the manifest but the driver and helper just laughed. He stayed with his rig for lack of anything better to do while he waited. There were two or three other rigs parked in the tunnel sharing his involuntary detention. Just in case they thought they might want to leave, three sentries were posted between them and the tunnel's entrance. Every now and then one would scowl in his direction. His ire, initially directed at the Army for having hijacked his load, slowly transferred to the sentries who prevented him from leaving. As he paced he became more and more agitated. About nine times he tried his cell phone but, either due to the volcanic fallout or the mountain's bulk, he was unable to connect.

    He knew Louisa would be out of her mind with worry. The last time they'd spoken was over sixteen hours ago. He had told her he would be home by now but he hadn't been able to talk to her to let her know what was going on. He thought of Raul, Esteban and Flor, his beautiful children. He was certain that Salt Lake City was experiencing the same fallout he was in Colorado Springs. It wrenched his guts to imagine his family riding out this storm without his support. He was well aware that there was nothing he could do to negate the power of God on Earth but Louisa needed his presence to stabilize herself. And the children leaned so heavily on her.... He felt he would go insane if he couldn't get home.

    In an attempt to calm his mind he climbed into the cab of his tractor and turned on the CB radio. The voices that came over the speaker were scratchy and spotty but it was at least some mode of communication. "Breaker 19," Agustin began. "Breaker 19, this is Durango Diego...how copy?"

    "Go ahead, Diego, you've got the Bearcat...how

copy?"

"Bearcat, Bearcat, this is Durango Diego. What's your 20 buddy?" He hated using this trucker's lexicon but if this communication network could possibly connect him to his family, he would force himself to get through it.

"I-25, buddy. Just north of C. Springs. What can I do for you?"

"Bearcat, I'm being held by the military and I need to get in touch with my family in Salt Lake. Can you get to a pay phone?"

"Pay phone hell, buddy! I've got my cell phone right here next to me!"

"Bearcat, can you please call my family for me? They were expecting me to arrive yesterday and I can't use my cell. The Army won't let me use a land line here…" he choked and almost sobbed," and Louisa needs to hear from me. Please Bearcat, can you call my family?"

"Diego, I'd be proud to help you out. How come you're messed up with the Army anyway?"

"They took my load…said it was for the government. Due to the emergency. Can you copy my number?"

"Course I can, Diego. I been hearing about that mess all day. Seems like about a third of the loads on the road have been hijacked by Uncle Sam."

Agustin rapidly passed the phone number and within a minute he heard Bearcat again. "Durango Diego, you got somebody here who wants to talk to you real bad.

Go ahead, ma'am." He then heard Louisa's sweet voice calling his name. "'Gusti? Agustin?"

They talked for about ten minutes when the truck began to drive out of radio range. Agustin was calling for Louisa but she was unable to hear him. Then a new voice broke in.

"Diego, you've got Long Haul Sally here. I've been listening in: It'd be my pleasure if I could help get you reconnected."

Agustin heard snatches of other truckers talking to Sally and he understood that Bearcat was now passing along Louisa's number. "Diego, it's Sally again. Your missus is back on the radio!"

The truckers spent the next hour playing handoff with Agustin and Louisa. The two were able to hold a remarkably private conversation despite its very public conveyance. Agustin promised that he would be home soon. They signed off with love to one another but in many ways it sounded as though they were saying their last goodbye.

Carmen Fletcher found herself back in a familiar role. Like the horror show she had left in Casper, she was playing medical doctor again. She and Mark had set up a triage of sorts and together they were working through the various injuries that had entered with the crush of people. Mark had actually resisted at first. He said that it was a bad idea to let the people know that they were doctors. To Carmen's utter disbelief he had said that Darwin was taking over; that the weak ones would self-eliminate if they would just be allowed to die. This callous approach appalled her and she stated as much unequivocally. It was only after many minutes of argument that he relented but was less than enthusiastic in the performance of his duties.

This group was much easier than the one back in

Casper. Although they had made their way to the mountain through the rock storm, remarkably few of them had any serious injuries. Mostly she saw lacerations and contusions. All the tough stuff she sent over to Mark who scowled as though she were personally responsible. In a way it was fortunate that they had to go through this exercise. They were able to find and identify all of the medical supplies in the underground base. The supply was quite good, although it was beginning to show signs of its advanced age. Since the DOD had decided to close Cheyenne Mountain's facility, upkeep of the long-term supplies had taken a back-seat priority.

There was a murmuring and commotion just down the hall from their small infirmary. The knot of noise and people came closer. Then General McIntyre separated himself and strode over to Mark.

"And this, Mr. President, is Doctor Mark Zorbas: Our physician in residence as well as my own personal doc."

The President stepped forward to shake Mark's hand. While having his hand pumped, the President looked askance at General McIntyre and asked pointedly, "You don't have enough good military doctors to care for your health, General?"

McIntyre flushed red while Mark did the same but for a different reason. "Mr. President, it is a genuine *honor* to meet you, sir! If there is anything I can do for you during your stay here…well…I'll do it! Yes, sir!"

Carmen rolled her eyes as Mark kowtowed and embarrassed himself. It brought back memories of Mark brown-nosing his professors for grades and plum assignments. "Guess that much hasn't changed," she thought.

"Doctor Zorbas, you just keep doing what you're doing right now. Something tells me that your skills are going to prove to be quite useful to this little group." He exchanged a quick glance with McIntyre. Not quick enough however, to be overlooked by Carmen. She mused on this for the remainder of the day, while busying herself with her patients' worries.

Until now the people of Jacksonville, Florida had remained relatively unaffected by events in the western half of the continent. The meteor strike had deposited tens of thousands of tons of material into the atmosphere but due to the upper airflow patterns, the lion's share had worked its way north of them. Likewise, when Yellowstone erupted, most of the ejecta had blown north. Now however, the flow around the globe was beginning to distribute more evenly. Within 72 hours of the Yellowstone eruption, ash and dust had circled the globe. The yellow smog-like haze they had seen off to the north was becoming darker by degrees.

As the ash, soil, rock and dust worked their way around the Earth, an uncomfortable darkness began to settle with it. The high, bright clouds of plume were reflecting the warming sunlight away from the planet. Plummeting temperatures accompanied the darkness. Three days after Mount Rainier blew, the normally 90 degree temperatures of Jacksonville were a decidedly chillier mid-50's...and dropping. Citrus crops were dying due to the overnight frosts and lack of sunlight. Tourists, the lifeblood of the state, were leaving in droves. The east coast was slowly accumulating an ash buildup that was choking its ability to exist.

Jacksonville was merely a bellwether for the entire world. It was the rare location that had anything close to resembling clear skies. The brown and gray pall had replaced the familiar blue as more and more fallout circulated.

Sunrise brought a pale imitation of day's light. Choking dust clouds blew everywhere. In the rainforests, ash and soot mixed with moisture and came down in great gobs of muddy goo. Rivers began to fill with the solid muck. Creeks became stopped with sludge and swamps formed spontaneously where once clear water flowed. Within a week of the asteroid's impact, the blue ball that was the Earth we know had become something completely different. And things would only get worse from here.

T he first few days in the mountain were tense. The military people were extraordinarily uneasy having all these civilians constantly underfoot. They'd all been briefed by the generals to allow unrestricted access. Unrestricted! That could only mean one thing: The temporary guests were about to become permanent. Rumors were rampant.

As for their civilian guests; the discomfort was at least equal. They'd run to the mountain seeking refuge—to save their own lives. Having accomplished that, they had no further purpose here. They were, nonetheless, prevented from leaving. So they had nothing to do but roam the halls of this most secure facility, poking around under the watchful and untrusting eyes of their own military.

At about ten in the morning on the third day the

leaders announced that everyone possible should gather in the Combat Operations Center's briefing area. Slowly the people filtered in. The room was now filled with as many chairs as could fit. The screens which had once displayed the security status of the U.S. forces were now all displaying the major news networks. The scenes were horrifying.

New York was blackened. The sky, the air...everything. No-one was venturing out on the streets. The few brave souls that did were forced to wear gas masks. Police and National Guard patrolled the streets. Shops were closed tightly. The reporters had to interview residents at the doors to their homes. The country's most populace city had ground to a standstill.

Los Angeles was similar, though it was still undeniably Los Angeles. There were a few shots of surfers struggling in the muddy ocean waters, wearing bandanas and dust masks. There was more activity in the street. Traffic was less than half of what L.A. faced daily. The paparazzi covered the occasional celebrity party with its devil-may-care participants. Alexis Coffey stifled a little cry when that story aired, no doubt regretting she couldn't have attended.

Another story was centered in Beijing. The city was less bad than the American cities shown but the sky was a dingy, dark yellow. Pedestrians were out and about. Everyone was wearing some sort of mask to block the pollutants. Bicycles were used extensively. The rarer automobiles appeared to have been stranded by the gunk in the air.

Finally all of the screens showed a single report from a station in Chadron, Nebraska. The station manager had sent a reporter and cameraman to get as close as they could to Yellowstone. They took footage of several towns along the way. Lusk, Wyoming, just across the border, had never been much of a town. Now it was abandoned. It appeared as though the few hundred residents had decided to desert en-masse. The only living creatures were a few magpies and a stray cat creeping through the village. Douglas was next along the route and its fate was almost identical to Lusk. The ash was noticeably deeper the further west the pair traveled.

Casper was the first town of any size they encountered. Ash was piled up to a dozen feet in some places. Where it fell without disturbance from the wind, it was four feet deep. Cars were stranded and abandoned everywhere. Bodies were identifiable under piles of dust and ash. The reporters took a long shot of the hospital: A doctor's white coat was visible in the distance, its owner draped over the hood of a vehicle. Carmen Fletcher covered her face and bolted from the room. The eeriest part of the town was the lack of movement. It was evident that nothing survived Yellowstone's blast.

The pair of newsmen made it as far as Powder River. They had to use a snowmobile to get that far. Even that machine gave out and they had to hike the last three miles into town. Actually, there was no town left. The camera recorded the closest thing to Dante's inferno ever seen on earth.

Stumps of trees smoldered in the blowing cinders. Massive chunks of glowing boulders rested everywhere. The darkness and soot were unbearable. The station relayed that the reporter had failed in that town. He died while trying to deliver his final account. The station was unable to show that report—the newsman coughed and choked up blood while attempting to deliver his last story. He hemorrhaged an artery in his lung and died within minutes. Although it was all caught on film, his death was too gruesome to publish.

The cameraman had hiked back out to where he could find another snow machine and had ridden that back to Casper. He was hospitalized when he got back to Chadron but didn't live three hours. His lungs had been seared, charred and sliced from the silica dust.

The anchor reporting the story was crying shamelessly as he told the tale of these two brave men who brought back the story from hell. There wasn't a sound from the crowd watching in the mountain. The TV remained on 24 hours a day and the room remained full.

Dennis Schweigert was wandering around the interior of the station when he happened on an Air Force officer sitting on the floor in a darkened hall. As Dennis was taking pains to pass without disturbing him, the officer looked up at him with hollow eyes. "You don't have to treat me like I'm dead," he said quietly.

"Sorry...?" Dennis was a little surprised when the man spoke and was caught off guard. "I just—" he stammered. "It's just that you looked like you'd prefer to be alone," he finally responded.

"Alone," said the man. "We're all going to be alone now, aren't we?"

Dennis had information from the top leaders which would verify that statement but he didn't particularly want to get into that specific discussion. He hedged, "Right now we're not alone, pal. Right now we've got a bunch of people working together for our survival."

"Without God," said the man. "What I mean is ALONE: As in 'abandoned by the Almighty.' That's what I meant."

Dennis wondered if he wanted to be having this discussion with this man at this particular moment. After a moment's thought he decided and then answered. "You know, I don't really have any place I need to be right now. You mind if I take a seat?"

"Free country..." said the officer morosely.

"So, Major? Sergeant? I still can't figure out all this rank stuff."

"Captain," said the man. "Captain Sandon. Call me Caleb."

"OK, Caleb. I'm Dennis. What's on your mind?"

"God," said Caleb without hesitation.

"God," repeated Dennis. "Well, I can tell you I'm not very well versed on the topic, but I could sure listen...."

Caleb started right in. "Just what the hell is God doing?" Shaking his head he said, "Please pardon my French but I'm pretty mad right now!" Dennis nodded for him to continue. Caleb went on. "God's blowing up the world. The end times are here. It is the hour of the triumphant return of our Lord." He sighed deeply and buried his face in his hands, elbows on his knees. "God took my son. Took him away from me right here. Right in the parking lot."

Any impulse that Dennis may have had to argue with the man, particularly the science of what was happening outside, was wiped away by that statement. He waited silently for Sandon to continue.

Sighing again, Caleb did continue. "I've waited my whole life for this. I've prayed, I've hoped, I've prepared. I've taught my family to anticipate this and to be ready when it happens. I just didn't expect that it would cost the life of my son." He laughed a bitter laugh. "God didn't falter when he lost *his* son though, did he?" Dennis had no answer and the two men sat in the quiet of the hallway for almost a minute.

"What do you do," Caleb wondered aloud, "when God doesn't keep his end of the bargain? What kind of alternative does one insignificant man have in a breach of contract with the Lord God Almighty?" Caleb stared at his hands clasped together between his legs. He looked at Dennis and said, "I mean, everything I've ever been taught tells me I should be riding triumphantly on the clouds into Heaven with my Lord and Savior. But so far that hasn't happened." Throwing his hands wide he almost shouted, "Was I not a good enough Christian? Have I somehow failed the Lord and now I'm to be left behind with the sinners?" Then he said abruptly, "What recourse do I have if the Supreme Being changes the rules at the last minute and I've wasted an entire life?"

Dennis was a little overwhelmed by the strength of this man's faith. The kind of conviction Caleb was displaying countered everything Dennis had taught or believed. He had had discussions with believers in the past and he was comfortable with his arguments of science. After all, what better proof could you possibly have than concrete, undeniable evidence? But the sheer intensity of Caleb's faith—the absolute, fundamental, unshakable nature of his belief—it had the power to impress even a hardcore disbeliever like Dennis. He respectfully waited for Caleb to say more.

"It's not fair. Damn it, it's not *fair!* My boy is dead!" Now Caleb was shouting. "He should be risen. The Rapture should be happening. Where is God??" He glared at Dennis with frightening intensity. "**WHERE—IS—GOD?**"

Dennis was completely stymied. In the first place he had only been transiting this hallway and had had no thought whatsoever of stepping into the middle of a theological conundrum. But he saw himself as a reasonable person and could easily sense the agony of this man's plight. So he made an attempt. "I think God is in your heart. I think he's where he's always been: In your love for your son." He quickly ran out of steam for this hopeless argument. "In your…heart," he finished weakly.

"That wasn't the deal!" spat Caleb, standing up menacingly. "I didn't spend my entire life preparing for the glory of the return of the Son of Man only to find that I'm supposed to be satisfied with some warm feeling in my heart! Bullcrap!

That wasn't the deal!" he cried, shaking his fist at the ceiling.

Alarmed, Dennis joined the ranting man by standing in the hallway. But his apprehension was unnecessary. Caleb threw up his hands and shouted once more, "That wasn't the deal!" He threw himself backward against he wall and slowly slid downward. Once again he was sitting pitifully alone in the hall, just as Dennis had found him. He whimpered one last time, "That wasn't…the deal," and then buried his face in his hands, totally alone in his grief.

Completely out of his depth and knowing he could do nothing to ease this man's pain, Dennis reached out slowly, touched Caleb gently on the shoulder and then, not knowing what else he could do, continued down the hall.

Karl Roscoe

General McIntyre was discussing a few management issues with the President when an airman stopped by the open door. "Excuse me, sirs," said the young man. "Have you seen General Grabowski? I found the extra mattresses and furniture he was looking for and stowed them in his quarters as requested."

"Extra mattresses?" inquired the President, raising an eyebrow at Mac.

"Don't look at me, Mr. President." He turned to the airman. "How many mattresses did the general order, son?"

"Four, sir. In addition to the one he already has."

"Thank you, airman. I'll inform the general as soon as he returns."

"Yes, sir," said the airman and walked off down the

hallway.

The President looked quizzically at McIntyre again. "Four *more* mattresses? Is he planning an orgy or what?"

"I suggest we ask the general, sir," said McIntyre nodding toward the door. General Grabowski was just coming in.

"Ask the general what, Mac?" said Grabowski genially.

"Ask the general what purpose he has in ordering four additional mattresses delivered to his quarters," said the President icily. "You are aware that accommodations are at a premium here in the mountain and they are not to be squandered on personal whim."

"Not a whim, sir," replied Grabowski testily. "I'm stowing them for future use, should the need arise."

"Seems to me that a storeroom might be a better place to keep them, general," stated the President.

"I'm afraid I have to agree with the boss, Bill," said McIntyre. "Hoarding is a bit unseemly in this situation."

Grabowski dug in his heels. "I'll do as I see fit with the available resources of this mountain. You'll recall, General McIntyre, that I have one star more than you and I will pull rank if necessary."

McIntyre registered his surprise quickly. "I didn't realize that seniority was going to be an issue here, *general*, but for the record I'd like to point out that this is still my command and until my command is relinquished, I'll be giving *all* the orders. Your extra star notwithstanding...." McIntyre was beginning to be irritated with this nonsense.

Before Grabowski could retaliate, the President broke in. "And both of you gentlemen would do well to remember that you are in my employ and serve at my pleasure."

McIntyre looked down and immediately said "Of course, Mr. President."

Grabowski looked contemptuously at the President and said nothing.

"General Grabowski? Do you have something you'd like to say?" asked the President.

"No, sir. I'll follow orders, *sir*," growled Grabowski.

"Good," said the President. "Now we have some issues to attend to that won't wait. I have to prepare an address for the people of this country, to let them know what is happening and what we plan to do. I want all the facts and I want them straight. General Grabowski, set me up with Schweigert as soon as possible." Grabowski glowered but nodded. "Mac, have your folks set up the broadcast equipment. I'm afraid that this is going to be quite unpleasant. If we're going to hold this nation together even for a short while, we'll need to put together one hell of a speech." Then he changed the subject. "Meanwhile, you two are going to have to get this mountain set up for the long haul. Get some staff together—we'll meet in half an hour in my quarters."

"Yes, sir," said McIntyre.

"Yeah," said Grabowski. "I'll be there," he sniffed

and stomped out of the room.

F or two solid days he'd been following her. He'd kept a respectful distance but was becoming bolder as he came to understand her movements. She was in the cafeteria with a mug of tea when he decided to approach her.

"Ms. Coffey? Hi, my name is Mark Zorbas. *Doctor* Mark Zorbas. It's a real pleasure to meet you." He held out his hand as if to shake hers.

Alexis looked at his hand as though it were leprous. She crossed her legs and looked in another direction.

"Um," said Mark, hand awkwardly dangling in space. "Uh, you mind if I sit down?"

Again she didn't answer and continued to look away.

Taking this as a positive sign, Mark pulled up the chair across from her. Two tables over were a couple of fans who'd seen this happen more than once in their short tenure in the mountain. "Watch, now" whispered one delightedly. "She's trying to come up with the ultimate kill!"

"So, like I said, my name is Mark. You can call me Mark, anyway..." he stammered. "I'm from here. Well, not here, here, but Wyoming. I went to school in Boulder—undergrad. Med school was someplace else but I'm kind of a native!" He laughed, a dry hollow sound in the silence. "So...are you enjoying your stay? Are they taking good care of you here?" Aware that he was babbling, he decided to change tack slightly and tried a new angle. "I'm kinda in good with the general who runs the place. I actually met the President of the United States yesterday...." He nodded to himself. "Cool," he said and laughed his dry laugh again.

"OK, I've noticed you haven't been around the inside of this mountain too much," he started again. "I've been all over in this place. Maybe I can give you a tour or something. I mean, if you want to look around the inside of this big secret place.... You know," he smiled, a big greasy grin.

She finally looked at him. She smiled back with her million-dollar dazzler and said "Do you know what I'd really like?"

Mark's face lit up as he said, "Name it!" Leaning into her he said, "Just tell me and it's yours!"

She lowered her voice to a whisper as she leaned forward conspiratorially. "I would like..." she began, "to be left the fuck alone." Mark was stunned. "Completely alone.

Blissfully alone. Nobody stalking me through my day, dodging behind corners every time I turn around. I would like," she went on, leaning back now and looking at the ceiling "to have a single day without some little cretin like yourself coming up as though you had an actual chance in hell of spending more than two minutes with me. Right now," she said looking directly at him without a trace of the former cheer, "I would love for you to drag your sorry, worthless ass back down whatever sewer it came from." She tossed her hair and looked back up at the ceiling. "And you can stay there. And rot." She shifted in her chair and sniffed over her shoulder, "Or whatever. Just leave me alone so I can drink my tea in peace. Got it?"

Mark was in shock. He knew that attempting to initiate a social connection with her was going to be a long shot but this was as far from his expectation as could possibly be. He sat openmouthed in front of Alexis, too horrified to move.

"That's fine," she said. "You just stay here then." She stood and turned away. "I'll find a place where you aren't." Leaning in close to his face she said, "Have a *really* nice day." Then she strode purposefully down the nearest hallway.

The fans at the nearby table were beside themselves with mirth. Slapping thighs and backs, they repeated the conversation line for line. "That was awesome!" they shrieked. The howling eventually pierced Mark's state of shock and he stood, face burning. After a moment's hesitation and, after choosing a very different direction, he slinked away.

Meanwhile, Alexis found herself walking back to the closed door of the mountain. Somewhere, she knew, on the other side of that door were thousands—maybe millions—of fans, just waiting for her return. "What a glorious day that will be," she mused. "They'll open that stupid door and out I'll walk. The cheers will be deafening. My comeback will be spectacular. I'll outshine every other Hollywood used-to-be! Alexis Coffey will be the only name America will ever want to hear!"

She would sit by that door and dream that same dream every day.

Washington D.C. was abuzz. The President was going to make an important announcement from inside of Cheyenne Mountain this evening. Special arrangements had been made for the western states' representatives. Due to the meteor and volcanoes, they had been unable to return to their constituencies. Places of honor were set up for representatives of Idaho, Wyoming and Washington State. Only a few of the representatives from the other states had taken advantage of the short travel window to return to their homes. Most of them had come back to D.C. immediately after checking in with their districts.

Challenges for this announcement and broadcast were much greater than usual. The maintenance engineers had been hard at work securing a dust-free environment for the joint session. Everyone knew that this would be a very important speech. No self-respecting Congressperson wanted to be left out of the occasion. Coordinators were expecting just-shy of a full house.

The city of Washington had taken quite a hit. Almost all communication lines had suffered after the multiple calamities. As a result, polling was unreliable. They had to return to the old-style politics of trusting your gut. No-one raised in the high tech world of instantaneous results was quite comfortable with old fashioned politicking so legislation had essentially ground to a halt. Of course, they had wasted no time in declaring emergencies and approving emergency spending bills, but with the world in such complete and utter chaos, not a single Senator or Congressman would dare to stand out in front with bold legislative initiatives for anything other than emergency aid.

The world was watching as well. All the world's leaders were attempting to contact the President on a daily basis, trying to decipher what the Americans would do with this impossible situation. Since they couldn't get hold of the President himself, they had to make do with the off-the-cuff advice of multiple staffers who were just doing their best to keep up with the hopeless nature of the circumstances.

Relief was the watchword for tonight's speech. Relief that the President of the United States was taking strong and positive action. Relief that he would chart a course to get America and the world moving in a positive and forward direction. Mostly though, it was relief that the burden of having to make decisions and set policy was being lifted from their shoulders and placed, rightly, on those of the President.

This tension was not limited to the capitol city, however. Anxiety had been building for some time within the mountain. People had been hearing bits and snatches of conversation and were trying to put together a picture of what the President would announce that night. Rumors, again, abounded. Everyone close to the leaders tried to pry out any information they could at every available opportunity. As Dennis had been heavily involved in the technical aspects of the speech, he found himself something of a local celebrity. People would bring him a cup of coffee unasked for while he sat in the galley. Some would initiate conversations as he passed them in the halls, as though they were old friends meeting again after a long separation. The fact was that the generals were both very busy men with important jobs to do and the President; well he was the President! So Dennis found himself being actively sought out for more conversational opportunities than he'd had in the previous six years. Eventually he found it easier to sit and wait in a small room, alone and with the door closed.

The President was to speak from the Combat Operations Center where they had set up several cameras. Every available seat in that room was filled. The anticipatory buzz reached a crescendo when he walked into the room and then a hush settled over the crowd. The President sat down behind an imposing desk, took a deep breath and then began.

"Fellow Americans:" he said, "Fellow residents of the planet Earth:" he adjusted his reading glasses. "Eight days ago a terrible calamity befell the citizens of Calgary, Canada. In the space of a few short seconds a previously unidentified asteroid, approximately three miles across, slammed into their city and destroyed it completely. The President of the United States was in Spokane, Washington at the time. He, along with a number of his staff, was killed in the aftermath of that horrible explosion. As you know, the meteor caused a tsunami throughout the Pacific, claiming many more lives. The next few days were inconceivably difficult for all of us. But the fallout from this disaster, it is my sad duty to inform you, is not finished yet.

"I am told by the finest minds in the scientific community that there was not a more unfortunate place on the planet for this asteroid to have hit. The waves of destruction radiated outward, shattering the Earth's crust as they propagated. These fractures led directly to the west coast of the U.S. and Canada. As a result of this fracturing, previously stable structures of the crust were shattered and long-dormant volcanoes sprung back to life. East and south of the impact the single largest super volcano on the planet, Yellowstone, exploded with a fury never witnessed by the eyes of modern man." He paused for a breath.

"Had the meteor struck in virtually any other location on Earth, we would have had weeks — perhaps years — of fallout. But it did not and it is my unfortunate task to tell you that we *will* not. We will not have years of fallout. Neither will we have decades. Our best estimates are that we are in for centuries of recovery. Already we are seeing temperatures plummeting worldwide. This trend will continue for many months. Our planet will soon lose an average of 70 degrees Fahrenheit, despite where you might live." He shifted his attention back and forth from his notes to the camera pointed at him.

"After a period of many months the ash and dust now clogging our air will fall to the ground and settle. The air will clear and the planet will begin warming once more. The warming will continue unabated and soon the Earth will become too hot for any living thing to survive. Water supplies will be contaminated by acid from the volcanic sulfides. Our home planet will be frozen, then baked and poisoned. The prospects for any life on Earth are grim and the prospects for human life are" he slowed as he said the next words, "almost non-existent." The audience in the room began to murmur again. "Ladies and gentlemen, fellow human beings: Our species is on the verge of extinction."

Off his notes now, he took off his glasses and looked steadily into the camera. "This is the most difficult thing I've ever had to say in my life." He tilted his head slightly and said, as if this was the first time it had occurred to him, "I realize that this is the most difficult thing any of you have ever had to hear." He let his notes fall flat on the desk before him and clasped his hands together. "The reign of man on this planet has come to an end." He shrugged his shoulders and looked down at his hands folded in front of him. Then, back up at the camera. "A small number of people are with me in this mountain. It is here, protected from the ravages of nature, that a single tribe of humanity will make an attempt at long-term survival. At the survival of our species. No-one in this place was chosen. We all ended up here rather by accident. It is by this natural lottery that this community will become humanity's best hope for survival. I have ordered the door sealed—no-one will leave, no-one will enter for a period of at least two years."

He looked down again and when he looked at the camera this time his eyes were full of tears; his voice thick with emotion. "I was made President of the United States by a freakish cosmic accident." He choked slightly and looked again at his clenched hands. After a moment he said, "I would not have chosen this path by myself. I would not have chosen to be with these people, in this mountain. If I were free to choose, I would be at home with my family. But it was my job which required my presence here and it is a second cosmic accident that is keeping me here even against my will." He shifted in his chair, his body tense and rigid.

"Libbie, my beautiful wife, we have had 31 of the most glorious years together. I don't think it possible that any man has ever loved a woman the way that I have loved you. My being trapped in this enclave while you are at home in Washington is the most unacceptable situation I've ever encountered." Tears were flowing freely down his face now. "Libbie, may the end be swift and merciful for you. May God almighty hold you closely and protect you with his love." Choking on emotion, he went on.

"Chloe, my firstborn, my beautiful daughter: You were right to pursue your own destiny. I love you so much yet I can't use words to express my feelings. Stay with Francis and the children now. Be certain to tell them all how much I love them."

Addressing his son he said, "Steven, I am proud of you. You have grown to be the man I've always hoped you'd be. Go home to your mother. She'll need your strength. All of you…go home to the ones you love. Tell them how much you love them. Be with them in your final hours. In the final hours of mankind. And may the merciful and loving God gather you all unto his breast and welcome you into his kingdom." He looked again at his clasped hands resting on the desk and, without looking at the camera, he ended. "Goodbye."

Karl Roscoe

I t was amazing. The world actually listened to the words of this one man. People did everything in their power to return to those they loved, to spend their last days together. News organizations began airing spots where family members could say goodbye to others far away. There was an unprecedented reaching out—a spirit of cooperation and help that had never existed in modern memory.

But it didn't last. After three or four days, denials began to be shouted out. The President was lying. The planet and its inhabitants would go on. There was no real proof that it was going to happen. Denial became anger. Large crowds appeared at the locked-down entrance to the mountain. There were jeers and demands made to be let in.

The first big incident was in Sao Paulo. Crowds of

rioting people stormed the national offices, looting, destroying property and beating any officials they could locate. Then, just outside of Fort Worth, Texas, a shouting match escalated into a shooting. This was followed by a retaliatory shooting and a six-hour gun battle erupted, quelled only by police and National Guard Troops. Eight people were killed in the violence. In Bonn, Germany, another rioting crowd burned everything in sight. Violence and pandemonium were breaking out everywhere.

In Hong Kong, troops were pushed aside by looters, taking every morsel of food available in the city. Train cars were a favorite target. People were literally killing each other over a box of crackers. Some had the foresight to go deep underground and hoard food and water supplies. There were a few places left that they might be safe for a few years.

Others simply gave up. There were many mass suicides. Families chose to die together rather than suffer the long, slow agonizing death that awaited everyone else. Building and bridge jumpers were everywhere. Bodies began to litter the cities, though it would be weeks before the affects of the fallout would take their full toll. Civilization was crumbling at its edges. Mankind was once again becoming just another animal.

The astronauts and cosmonaut aboard Unity had been a week now with no contact from Houston. During the initial two weeks of the calamity communications had been steady and reliable. Then gaps began to appear. Scheduled communications went unanswered. Apologies were offered by controllers and understood by the station's occupants. Gaps grew wider as more and more mission controllers failed to show for work. Finally there were no more transmissions at all.

The mood on board had grown dark in lockstep with the blackening Earth below. Unity's team, captivated by the initial blast from Yellowstone, had watched as the world — their world — literally disappeared. Initially the northern half of North America was blanketed in dusty smog and vanished. This took place over the course of a single week. Gradually the dark stain spread over the southern hemisphere and within three weeks the entire globe had gone from a beautiful blue and white gem to a blotchy gray and black shadow.

Kasparof commanded Unity's crew to continue with their scientific duties; more to occupy their time than to provide lasting advances to humankind's pool of knowledge. The crew complied with neither fight nor question, silently understanding the commander's intent. DiGiammo and Narita attempted to immerse themselves in their assigned duties but were only partially successful. Even for these disciplined professionals, thoughts of suffering families could not be held at bay. Now, five weeks into the disaster, they had completely given up on even the pretense of work. Their time was spent with the radio, trying to find someone…anyone who could talk back.

It had become an intensely frustrating task. Radio communications were severely hampered by events on the surface. The frequencies used by NASA were proprietary — ordinary citizens didn't have access to them. Even those who could be reached didn't bother to answer. What were the travails of three men in space when the destruction of the earth was at hand?

It was Narita who had hit on the idea of trying to contact Cheyenne Mountain. They pursued this new goal enthusiastically and attempted contact every thirty minutes for two days. For two days they received only radio silence and static in return. Disheartened by the response, their efforts were reduced to sporadic attempts based on mood and desperation. Then, unexpectedly, a clear, lucid response came through.

Karl Roscoe

Caleb Sandon was holding Leah's hand in both of his. He was crying. "I don't understand it," he said. "Why hasn't he come? Where is Jesus?"

Leah looked with pity on the man she loved. He had been like this since Joshua's death: Broken. A mere shell of the tower-of-strength she had known. She reached out to caress his face. "Caleb," she said softly, "what if He *doesn't* come? We have to be prepared to go on. We have to find strength for our children's sake." She pulled his chin upward to look directly into his eyes. "*I* need you here and now. The children need you here and now. There will be a time for grieving for Joshua but right now we need to think about how to move forward."

"Impossible!" he cried. "How can you even dare to

think that He won't come? Our Lord would never forsake us." He was quiet for a moment. "He would never forsake us, would He?" he pleaded with more than just a tinge of desperation in his voice. His eyes searched Leah's deeply. In them Leah saw nothing of the man she had married. There was only a mannequin left. Haunted, empty. He was incapable of comprehending what she was asking him. His only focus was on the loss of his religious conviction. He would not, could not, function again until someone gave him the reassurance he sought.

With so little to do in the mountain, computer terminals were extremely popular. The internet continued to operate as long as there was power to allow the sites to publish. The mountain's residents found pockets of resilience where resourceful humans managed to survive the hellish conditions outside and blog their experiences. Not only were they able to survive in a seemingly impossible environment but they managed to keep their terminals and servers somehow supplied with power.

Thus the Cheyenne survivors were able to experience some of what the outsiders were having to endure just to stay alive. For the most part the Cheyenne group could only stand a little of that intensity before they shifted their attentions to more trivial considerations—in an attempt to escape the pervasive awareness of their confinement. They would while away hours at a time searching for entertaining snippets: Recipes, travel logs or just pretending to shop online. As the months underground progressed, the number of outside survivors dwindled as they lost power sources, food and the will to live. More and more the blogs detailing daily travails became the only thing left. The internet was dying as the gatekeepers who tended it slowly perished.

In the early days of their confinement many of the Cheyenne survivors would establish contact with the outsiders. Those inside sent messages of hope and support, trying to provide some sort of respite for those trapped on the outside.

The stories were horrific. The noxious cloud of ash and gas circled the globe quickly, killing hundreds of thousands. As the permanent darkness descended, the daily toll began to reach into the millions. Almost no manmade structure was safe. Underground was virtually the only refuge and, like Cheyenne Mountain, the only places capable of handling large numbers of people for extended periods of time were government owned or military complexes.

For a while they tracked the progress of a research station 150 feet below the waves of the Pacific Ocean. Rationing their supplies and power, they had managed to hold out for more than two months. They were able to maintain contact with the outside world for most of that time and relayed their observations of the effects of the cataclysm on undersea life. The results were not surprising: The darkness caused massive die-offs of phytoplankton. Without a base for the food chain, species began dying off one by one and then in droves. Near the end of their record keeping, they began to note a downward trend in the ocean's temperature, putting further stress on an already crippled system.

Elsewhere small bands of survivors holed up to try to wait it out. Some were unable to obtain enough food and water for the long haul and underwent torturous declines into oblivion. Others were unable to maintain social order and, despite having the necessary tools for long-term survival, managed to kill one another anyway. In the end, only a handful of small bands in Japan, Argentina, South Africa and the Ukraine were able to push through to the long haul.

The survivors in these far-flung locations all followed the same pattern established by the Cheyenne group: Initiate communications with those on the outside, offer them hope and support, witness their deaths via the internet and then recoil and try to find what distractions they could to blot out the reality of what was happening to their world. As the survival groups discovered one another, they found that they would communicate only with one another, in an attempt to insulate themselves against the horrors outside. Within a year these ties would be broken as networks failed, leaving the residents to silently wish each other luck in the difficult years to come.

Karl Roscoe

"You have to participate," insisted Carmen Fletcher. "Listen, you have nothing physically wrong with you. You have to eat. We've only been in here eight weeks — you're going to have to get serious about survival. You have to will yourself to live!"

The Latino man sat passively in front of her, hands flat on his thighs, eyes focused on infinity.

"Hello! Are you in there? Come on, pal. Give me something to work with. How about your name? What's your name?"

"Maybe he doesn't speak English," said a voice behind her. "Pardon my intrusion but maybe the guy just doesn't speak English." Dennis Schweigert was entering the makeshift infirmary and witnessed the exchange.

"Oh," said Carmen a little defensively, "and you'll miraculously bring him back with a few words?"

"Perhaps..." said Dennis. "I mean, it's worth a try, isn't it?"

"OK, go ahead," she snipped with a toss of her head. "See if you can get him to talk."

Dennis took a moment to scowl at her and then he said "Señor, queremos ayudar."

The man slowly came back from wherever he was and said "Help? You want to help me?"

"Yes!" said Carmen. "Yes we want to help you. Can you tell us your name?"

"Como se llama?" repeated Dennis. "What is your name, friend?"

"My name," said the man "is not important." His eyes focused again on that far away place. "It was important once. My children were going to carry my name. My wife was proud to call my name her own. Now..." he trailed off.

"Now what?" said Carmen. "Engage with me, sir. Please."

The man sighed deeply. "My name" he said, "is Agustin Sanchez. And my family is dead. All of them." He looked squarely at Carmen. "And I couldn't stop that. But worse: I couldn't even be with them at the end." A silent tear rolled down his cheek. "I couldn't even die with my wife and children." He shook his head sadly. Then he looked at Carmen and said with harsh anger, "And you want me to *engage?* You want me to stay with you in this unholy cave, to try to survive? For what? What purpose will it serve for me to live, knowing that my whole family waits for me in Heaven?" He whispered, "Dios..."

Dennis looked at Carmen. "Agustin," she said firmly, "you aren't the first man to experience this kind of loss."

Agustin laughed a bitter bark.

Undeterred, Carmen continued. "Agustin, it's important to understand your grief. You must understand there are phases you'll go through. There is a path. Others have been down it before. And there is light at the end. There is hope." Carmen was feeling more comfortable now that Agustin was interacting with her. She could use her training as a psychiatrist to finally help the man.

"Hope!" Agustin spat. "Did you not hear our President? There is no hope!" Agustin was alternating between his far away place and arguing with Carmen. "*No* man has ever had to endure such a loss. And you give me hope! Why don't you just let me die?"

"Agustin," said Carmen. "Agustin, talk to me!" she insisted. But he was gone. The far away black hell he had created for himself had claimed him and he would not return.

"Agustin?" Dennis tried. But it was no use. He would not come back. Dennis looked at Carmen again. "Um, Doc?"

"He's retreating," she said. "Emotionally withdrawing to protect whatever sanity he feels he has left. It's gonna take some finesse to draw him back out."

Dennis noted the soft cascade of her auburn hair, tumbling down from her high forehead. "Right now, you mean?" he asked.

"What?" she replied, distracted. "No, not right now. This is a long-term process. I can't fix it on the first try." She roused herself from her distracted concentration. "Why do you ask?" she said, not altogether genially.

"I don't know," he stumbled. "'Cause you look like you could use a break, I guess."

"What?" she repeated.

"A break," he said weakly. "You've been at this for a while, I'm guessing," he said looking around the thrown-together room. "How about a timeout for the Doc? Would you like to go get a cup of coffee or something?" He wasn't used to casually asking women out on a date, and current circumstances didn't make things easier. "I hear the canteen is making a killer cup now...."

"I don't even drink coffee," she snapped. Then, looking at Dennis' disappointed face she realized what he was asking. "Oh!" she said and looked away. "Oh," she said again, touching her hair and patting her pockets. "Uh, sure! Coffee sounds great. Or tea." They both shifted uncomfortably in the silence. "You know..." she laughed, "I could actually use a nice belt right now. Got any high-level connections you could massage?"

Dennis smiled in return. "I think I could probably use one too. And I know just where we can get it. Shall we?" He held out an arm indicating the doorway and she passed through, feeling for the first time in a very long time, something other than bleak helplessness.

Karl Roscoe

Caleb had gone off again to ponder his fate leaving Leah Sandon with the children. With Joshua's death the children had all grown closer. Jacob had become their de-facto father since Caleb's virtual disappearance and, sensing her need to sort things out for herself, Jacob steered the other children toward activities that would free her for time alone. It was during one such time she found herself face to face with a small, mousy woman.

"Excuse me," said the woman timidly. "Aren't you Leah Sandon?"

"Yes," said Leah, puzzled that the stranger would know her by name. "Can I help you?"

"I was hoping so," said the woman quietly. I'd like to ask you...I'd like to ask about your loss. About your son. I mean, if I may. I know how painful it must be and if I'm prying..." she trailed off, but looked hopefully at Leah's face.

"My loss...? My son...?" Leah couldn't keep the shock from her face or voice. "Why...? How...?"

"Oh," said the woman. "We all know. I'm sorry but you just can't keep tragedy to yourself in a small place like this. Everyone knows."

Recovering a little of her composure, Leah fell back on politesse. "Of course," she smiled, with some difficulty. "I'd love to tell you about my son."

The woman began again. "Actually, it's less about him and more about you. You seem so strong—so self-assured. How can you do it? How do you go on?"

Leah felt her guts churn but she steeled herself. "You just do," she said firmly. "It's not a thing you plan for. It's not a thing you find yourself waking up every morning promising to yourself—that you'll get through. You just go on because you have to."

The woman looked down. "I lost my family. My husband and two sons. They're," she nodded, indicating the town below, "...out there. And I'm in here. I don't know if they're alive right now. I only know that they're out there and I'm in here."

"Oh, my poor dear!" said Leah. "Oh, you've lost everyone and I've lost *only* one. Oh my dear friend, I am so sorry." She reached out and drew the woman toward her. "Oh my sweet dear, I am sorry for being so selfish."

The woman slowly crumbled into her embrace, first weeping, then collapsing and openly sobbing. She clung to Leah even tighter and poured the full weight of her grief into her. Leah accepted her completely and held her for a long time. When the woman had unleashed most of her tears, she pulled away self-consciously and began scrubbing her stained cheeks with her shirtsleeves. Leah kept her hand on the woman's back.

"I don't know!" the mousy woman said, raising both hands into the air. "I don't know if they're dead or alive. I don't know why I am in here and they are out there. Who decides these things?" She shook her head.

After a short silent break she began again. "I'm glad I'm in here," she said firmly. "Heaven knows I would rather be with my family in the end but, God forgive me, I'm glad to be in this mountain." She glanced at Leah with reddened, puffy eyes and confessed, "I've left them to die out there." She examined her wet cuffs as she spoke, now unwilling to look at her. "What is wrong with me? How is it that I could choose safety, knowing that it would cost my whole family to keep me alive?"

Leah fought to remain impassive. She wanted to hear the woman finish speaking without imposing her own sense of growing horror on the situation.

"Am I evil?" said the woman. "Will I survive on earth only to go to hell for leaving my family when I got scared?" The woman was letting it all out, now. "I was driving to pick up Ricky at football practice when the rocks started coming down from the sky. I was frightened! Nothing like this has ever happened before! This was the safest place I could think of to come so I drove straight up the road."

She sobbed again as she relayed the rest of the story. "I had to drive right by his school to get here. I can still see him in his helmet and pads standing there looking at me while I drove past him." She barked out a hoarse laugh. "He was wearing his helmet and shoulder pads to protect him from the rocks! He was waiting for me to take him to protection!" She was crying again but this time Leah did not move to embrace her.

"I've abandoned them! Dear God, I'm guilty. Guilty! And I wish I could feel bad for it. I feel worse for not even feeling bad."

Leah kept her hand lightly on the woman's back while she vented. This was a most stunning confession—the darkest, ugliest secret she had ever heard. She wanted to vomit...to scream in this woman's face. What a monster she was! To leave her own most precious family for the purpose of saving her own life? What possible value could there be in an action which could only devalue the life it saves? But she refrained, biting back the vile words as they formed in her throat. Instead she stroked the woman's hair, offering the only comfort she could.

The woman talked for half an hour longer and Leah

just listened. She poured a lifetime of regret out onto Leah, who accepted it all without comment. When she was finished, she thanked Leah. She told her how much better she felt. And Leah was shocked, confused and — just a little bit — pleased. Pleased that she had not vomited or punched this horrible woman. Pleased that she was able to listen and provide support. Leah was discovering a new and different part of herself. One that she felt she might like to get to know better.

Colonel Wilkes was the third officer General Grabowski had sought out that afternoon. "Jack, I want to thank you for stopping in to chat," began Grabowski.

"To be completely honest, sir, it's not like I had anything else to do...." responded Wilkes frankly. "Ten short months in this place and I'm worked completely out of a job."

Grabowski laughed and slapped Wilkes on the shoulder. "I like you, Jack," he said, shaking his head. "I like you!" Then he took a more serious tone. "And I trust you, Jack." Grabowski looked him in the eye. "I need men I can trust around me."

"Thank you, sir," said Wilkes, wondering where this was going.

Suddenly the door burst open and a handsome fiftyish woman walked in. "Oops!" she smiled. "Bill, you didn't tell me you'd be entertaining."

General Grabowski stood. "Jack, I'd like you to meet my wife: Cookie. Cookie, this is Colonel Jack Wilkes."

"Mrs. Grabowski," said Wilkes standing. "It's a pleasure to meet you." He looked quizzically at Grabowski. "I didn't think..." he said choosing his words with care, "...that you'd be able to join us here in the mountain."

She laughed girlishly and, with a wink said, "My Bill! I guess he pulled a few strings in the right places. And here we all are!"

"All?" queried Wilkes.

"The whole Grabowski clan!" she chirped. "I don't know how he does it," she said wrapping her arm into Grabowski's, "but he always seems to have some way."

Grabowski smiled into her beaming face. "Cookie, the Colonel and I have some important things to discuss. Could we have a few minutes?"

"Of course," she replied. To Wilkes she said, "It seems Bill is always cooking something up!" Grabowski patted her hand and she left the room with a little wave.

"Nice lady," stated Wilkes evenly.

"Yes," said Grabowski. "The best."

"You know," continued Wilkes gazing at the general, "I thought the President had restricted the mountain to current occupants only."

Grabowski matched the Colonel's stare. "As a matter

of fact, that's exactly what I wanted to talk to you about."

"OK, General," said Wilkes. "I'm listening."

"Jack, things are changing. Have changed already. The world has become a smaller place. So small, in fact, that you can fit almost everything that matters into a single mountain base." Wilkes waited for him to continue while Grabowski paced and weighed what he would say next. "The United States...the population of the United States has been reduced to what; fifteen? Sixteen hundred people? The same people who are now inside this mountain with us. So where does that leave the President? What happens to the authority of that President? And the Constitution from which that President derives his authority.... What are we to think of that document under our current circumstances? Does a contract written over two centuries ago have the capacity...the ability even, to address the current world situation?"

"With due respect General, you're dancing around the issue. Why don't you just tell me what's on your mind."

"Fine. What's on my mind, Jack, is just this: Desperate times call for desperate measures. I can't imagine a more desperate situation for America. For the world. For humanity. Our current situation calls for leadership. Strong, unequivocal leadership. *Proven* leadership." He stopped in front of Wilkes to present his next statement directly. "Our Vice President..." he smiled a smug, self-conscious smile. "Excuse me, our *President* has had precious little time and experience with the job. I'd be negligent in my duty to the people if I didn't question his ability to lead us through these extraordinary times."

"And," said Wilkes, "does the General have any idea *who* would be an appropriate leader to guide us through this crisis?"

"Someone with proven leadership experiences," said Grabowski. "Someone with legitimacy and credibility. Someone," he said with a meaningful eye on Wilkes, "who has a staff in place to carry a small band of survivors into a successful future. And those staff members can count on being the next generation of leadership. The second wave for this new Noah's ark."

Wilkes contemplated in silence.

"What do you say, Jack?" asked the general.

"I say..." answered Colonel Wilkes, "that it would be inappropriate for me to respond without the benefit of a great deal of thought. Under normal circumstances, I'd consult with my wife but, as you are aware, she is not here with us." Grabowski looked at the floor. "These matters you bring up are all very grave, sir. Very serious. I would be derelict in *my* duties to the Constitution, to the President...to the Republic, if I were to answer without careful consideration."

"I understand, Jack," said Grabowski, extending his hand. Altering the subject slightly he chided, "I guess I don't need to remind you that this conversation is necessarily classified until such time as it needs to be disclosed?"

"Of course, sir," said Wilkes. "I understand completely. I'll get back to you with my decision as soon as I make it."

"I'm confident you'll make the right choice, Jack. And I look forward to having you on my...on *our* team."

Having learned much from his humiliation, Mark Zorbas was much more cautious around Alexis Coffey. Though he cognitively acknowledged her rejection, he found that he was unable to accept that he had been spurned and he slipped slowly into an obsessive fixation.

He wanted to trace her every move. Realizing that he would not be able to physically follow her around the base without raising her suspicions or awareness, he found other ways to track her activities. Cheyenne Mountain had an extensive video surveillance network which he put to work immediately. The military people were now unconcerned about security so he found he could access and use the surveillance system with relative ease and privacy. Obviously, he couldn't spend days at a time in front of the monitors without attracting someone's attention, so he insinuated himself into a network of Alexis watchers. He had no trouble getting these people to report on her whereabouts and pastimes. As there was nothing to occupy their time in the installation, gossip was becoming a staple for the residents. Alexis made a natural target for these watchers and Mark was able to keep fairly close tabs simply by checking in with the various tongue-waggers.

For her part, Alexis was quite simply not that difficult to follow. Each morning she'd wake up, eat, take a short walk around the mountain and then go sit by the door. Sometimes she'd read a book or find another way to kill time. Mostly though, she would sit close to the entrance, imagining how wonderful it was going to be to emerge to the cheering fans, just waiting for her triumphant return. The wistful look on her face revealed her deepest thoughts.

Occasionally she would allow one of her fans to sit with her and she'd talk to them for an hour or so. Inevitably growing tired of their adulation and company, she would rudely dismiss them and spend the remainder of the day staring at the immobile door, nursing a black funk.

These brief meetings were like gold for Mark. Gleaning all he could from each detail, he was able to piece together a complete picture of her life. Sadly, he could have gotten as much information from the dog-eared, thumbed-through issues of the tabloids sitting in the canteen and break rooms. Alexis Coffey was *exactly* who she appeared to be: A shallow, self-absorbed, narcissistic party girl, with little or no ambition to be or become anything else. Her entire sense of self-worth rested upon reading about herself in the weekly gossip rags and ignoring crowds of cheering fans while entering the trendiest clubs.

Drawing deeper into his obsession day by day, Mark was able to effectively ignore that the object of his affection was nothing more than a cardboard cutout of a human being.

As the weeks underground progressed he found that his medical services became more and more in demand. There were abrasions, contusions, a broken finger, upset stomachs, some bruised ribs from a fight that broke out, one pacemaker problem and a curious Mexican man who was apparently trying to starve himself to death.

Under ordinary circumstances Mark would have welcomed the distraction that his work afforded him. With Alexis' presence however, he found that his profession was taking away from his obsession and he began to withdraw — to become unavailable when he heard about accidents or injuries.

The only person who knew Mark well enough to notice his change in behavior was Carmen Fletcher and, aside from one passing remark to a volunteer assistant, she was far too busy with her own distractions — trying desperately to save Agustin from his suicidal slide and the giddy hopeful sparkle of a new romance — to pursue the issue beyond that one comment.

So it was that Mark Zorbas began to conceive of a plan to win Alexis' heart. In his mind's eye he saw himself rescuing her from the tedium of their voluntary imprisonment. Initially she would be grateful but soon that gratitude would blossom into a deep and abiding love for him. He knew that, given a chance, she would see that he was the one man; the only man for her.

Edison Palmer had had a pretty good life. More accurately, Mr. Palmer had had an easy life. At the age of thirty-two he found himself employed as the Special Assistant to the President of the United States. Not that he'd done anything in particular to earn the position. Fact was that he'd never really done anything to earn anything.

Edison was the only son of Wendell Earl Palmer, oil and rail titan. Wendell's story was that of the classic rags-to-riches success. He started as a penniless orphan who clawed his way into the upper class. Once there, he discovered an uncanny knack for shrewd investment. He foresaw the energy crisis of the seventies and bought in just before prices went through the roof. The computer revolution was his next accurate prediction and his ground floor investments rode the crest of the tech wave. As his fortune was rising with these interests, he dabbled in railroad acquisitions and consolidations. Dabbling soon became major share control in the industry and, returning to oil, he amassed a diversified fortune which allowed him to become one of the best connected and most politically powerful men alive.

It was a direct result of that power and influence that placed Edison in the White House when the meteor hit. And it was that power and influence that kept him close by the new President's side during the transition and inauguration.

Let it be said for the record that Mr. Palmer was not a dumb man. He had graduated with a degree in Political Science from Boston University (Dad had wanted him to attend Amherst College). He'd done well enough—certainly not the Magna Cum Laude that his father had expected but neither a slouch.

Mr. Palmer the senior had arranged for an acceptance into Yale's graduate program—something Mr. Palmer the junior could never have pulled off on his own and that he was wise enough to recognize for the gift it was. Following grad school he was placed in a series of politically important positions at the local level which led to an appointment at the national level; culminating in his current position in the Presidential administration.

Not having personally earned anything on his own, Edison was fascinated by those who were set apart from the average. He first collected stories and experiences with the political elite...until he realized how shallow and short-sighted these people were. Next he pursued relationships with sports personalities. "Glorified Ghetto," he decided that these criminals with contracts should be called.

Celebrities were now the answer. Having come up short in his previous two quests, Mr. Palmer had decided that celebrities from Hollywood and the music world must possess the "certain something" that would instruct him in the nuances of life in front of the camera.

Sadly, his epiphany came at exactly the same time that the meteor collided with the planet and severely restricted his options for more research. By stroke of pure chance and fortune, he had been delivered an honest-to-God Hollywood star for up close and personal inspection. Right here in the mountain. He would acknowledge this opportunity and proceed with prudence and care. To tell the truth, he was not prepared psychologically for another failure of his theory of "otherness" and planned to give it every chance to succeed with Alexis Coffey. He would approach her carefully and she would share with him the secrets of the innate celebrity. Given their time underground, he would be able to study her for an extended period.

He began by observing her activities within the mountain. But, unlike the predatory designs of Mark Zorbas, his observations were based more on the naturalists "observe in the habitat" model. Mr. Palmer was unobtrusive enough as to be completely unnoticed by Alexis.

It was a follow-up on a report of a change in her whereabouts that led him to the room where the only operating radio was left on in the mountain. And that was where he heard the sound of Antonio DiGiammo's voice coming from the small speaker, with not even a trace of hope left.

"Cheyenne Mountain, this is Unity station. Come in please. Cheyenne Mountain, Unity calling. Come in...."

Mr. Palmer looked around in a panic. He had no experience with radios and would never locate the transmitter without help.

"Cheyenne, this is Unity station. Come in please.... Come in Cheyenne, this is Unity."

Edison Palmer began running down hallways, calling for help. "RADIO!" he shouted. "There's someone on the radio! Who knows how to work the damn thing?? There's someone calling us on the radio!"

He was barreling along at top speed when he rounded a corner and crashed headlong into the lifeless body of Caleb Sandon dangling from the overhead pipes by his official Air Force blue belt. Bouncing off the now-swinging body left Mr. Palmer sprawled on the hallway floor where he found the suicide note dropped by Caleb.

A pair of Security Policemen stood outside the door. General McIntyre was inside talking with General Grabowski.

"This is bullshit, Mac," said Grabowski.

"That's your opinion Bill and, so far, you're still welcome to it."

"What the hell is that supposed to mean?" snapped Grabowski.

"It means," said Mac quietly and evenly "that the Constitution of the United States of America does not get suspended. Regardless how extraordinary the circumstances. It means," he continued, "that the President is the legitimate representative of the people...no matter how many or how few remain. And," he said facing Grabowski directly, "it means that the petty ambitions of one individual with an overly inflated ego will supersede neither the needs nor the will of the people."

"Wilkes!" seethed Grabowski. "I never should have trusted that little turd."

"Colonel Wilkes had his objections to your designs on a dictatorship, yes. But he wasn't alone—not by a long shot." Mac softened for only a moment. "What in the Christ did you have in mind, Bill? Do you have any idea what people are thinking? What people are saying?"

Grabowski set his jaw and didn't answer.

"So that's it, is it?" McIntyre shook his head in disappointment. "Fine. Have it your way. The President has called a meeting for this afternoon. The people of this community will decide your fate. And that of your family as well."

Grabowski spat "You leave my family out of this!"

"You brought your family into this," returned McIntyre sharply. "Not a very popular decision, I might add. Now it's time for the people to decide what they want to do about it."

Grabowski turned his back on McIntyre.

"Three o'clock, Bill. The Security Police will escort you when it's time. Meanwhile you're under house arrest." He walked through the open door and then stopped with a final thought. "Just *try* for a little contrition. It may be your only chance to stay."

Grabowski didn't budge. The SP's closed the door, each taking a position on either side and staring forward in stony silence. When McIntyre was well out of earshot one of them spoke.

"What do you think?" he murmured.

"What?" responded the other.

"What do you think?" repeated the first.

"They don't pay me to think," said his partner. "I just follow my orders."

"Would you have gone along with him?" asked the first with a nod toward the closed door.

"I don't know…" answered the other, irritated. "What difference does it make?"

"A pretty big one to me. I swore an oath to protect and defend the Constitution and this guy was going to try to hijack that. Personally I hope they chuck him *and* his family out there."

"Orders from him, orders from that other general…what difference does it make?" he repeated.

"A lot to me," reiterated the first. "What this guy is trying to do is treason. That's punishable by death."

The other, engaging now, turned to face his partner. "You realize they're gone. All of them. They're all dead out there. There is no America. There are no Americans. We're it. All of humanity. And when we open that door, it'll be our turn to die. I'm pretty sure that that's one special little hell just waiting for all of us. You think we're gonna last for a year out there? So what do I care about treason?"

The first was thoughtful for a moment. "I think that's *exactly* why it's important. If we give up now... on what humanity has achieved, it will all have been for nothing. Think of the thousands of years it has taken for us to come up with an idea like freedom. And a piece of paper as remarkable as the Constitution. Even if it *is* our turn to go, we can still live the last of our lives the way we've earned to live. We can still embody the freedoms that mankind has striven for all these millennia."

Just guard the door like you've been told, Socrates," drawled the other. Returning to his position flanking the door, he said "Leave it to the big boys to do the heavy thinking."

Frustrated, the first turned back to his post and continued his thoughts. On the other side of the door the general, who had been listening to the exchange, found himself doing exactly the same thing.

Caleb had been dead for a week. Leah felt as though she'd been kicked repeatedly in the stomach. It seemed as though each time she'd had the figurative chance to take a breath, another kick arrived. Her mind lay gasping and numb at the totality of her loss.

Leah had been born into a fundamentalist family with a brutally strong father. His word was ironclad and no-one ever questioned him. Her mother had instructed Leah and her four sisters on the finer points of proper deferential behavior. Her two brothers became as their father: Tyrants in their own right.

Leah was a high school senior when she met Caleb. He was going through Air Force Officer Training School in her hometown of San Antonio, Texas. It was love at first sight for both. The transition to married life was remarkably easy for Leah. She simply moved from her father's home and care into her husband's. Almost nothing had changed except her address.

The children came immediately. Caleb was a firm believer in spreading the gospel via sheer mass. What better solution than repopulating the world with your own image and likeness? He ran his house like a military operation. She was the support and framework upon which he hung his values and beliefs. It was a fairly simple and straightforward arrangement: Caleb made all decisions regarding finance, family and life. He took his cue from their local pastor and the focus, he felt, remained firmly on God.

And now all that was gone. Her beautiful Joshua was gone. Caleb, the backbone of her whole world was gone: Taken by his own hand. Despair had claimed his life and the focus of her own life. Now what were her options? Could she, like Caleb, abandon her own young family? Four children depended on her more completely than anyone had ever experienced. These children were, quite literally, the future of the human race. Could she possibly cast off her own life and walk away from that?

What of her faith? Caleb had made a valid point. Where *was* Christ? Her whole adult life had been a mirror of Caleb's. Now that the end times were here, where was the Savior? Was it possible…*could* it be possible that the Bible was nothing more than a story? That Jesus wouldn't return in glory to carry them all away to heavenly reward? These blasphemous thoughts crowded in against a lifetime of devotion, each vying for her conscious consideration.

Before, she would just ask Caleb and he would give her a simple answer. But Caleb was no longer here. Neither was his simple and strong reassurance. Now Leah needed to make her own decisions based on what *she* knew—what *she* believed. And she asked herself: What did she know? What did she believe? What is faith to a woman who has had everything she ever valued taken away from her?

The others were still coming to see her, seeking her strength. But what strength did she possess without Caleb? She sought to help. She longed to receive the aid and comfort that others were getting from her. How could they not know? How could they not see her bare soul, exposed in front of them all? Her fears, her lack of experience in the world, her total dependence on one man; exposed like bleached bones in the desert. And yet they came. These people were strengthened by her words of comfort. They took this strength and passed it on to others. Then still others came.

What could she tell them? She shared what she felt about God but mostly she listened. The people responded. They told her they could feel the hand of God upon them when she spoke. It was confusing, upsetting, exhilarating. To be a channel for God's love…could it possibly be that she had been a teacher all this time…just waiting to step out of

Caleb's shadow and bloom?

Then it all became clear to her. Leah was as close to God as she had ever been. These people craved spiritual guidance. She would be their guide. She would lead them through this wilderness. And with the help of God they would all make it through.

General Grabowski stood by the open door of his quarters. His two door guards escorted him on the short walk to the Operations Center briefing room. The murmur and buzz that filled the room died immediately when he walked in. General McIntyre stood front and center with the President, next to an unoccupied chair—obviously waiting for Grabowski. He stiffened his spine, squared his jaw and marched smartly to stand in front of the chair.

The air in the room was electric. A hundred and eighty or so people were able to crowd into the room and scores more lined the hallways radiating outward. This was a big deal. They held their collective breath and waited for the proceeding to begin. General McIntyre started the trial.

"Ladies and gentlemen," he began, "we have a grave

situation before us, and with that situation comes a remarkable responsibility. Today you will hear the testimony of several officers who have brought forward evidence which implies an act of treason, planned against the President of our nation.

"The United States," continued the President on his cue, "has a proud tradition of assuming an individual's innocence until irrefutable proof of that individual's culpability is presented. Historically we have depended upon the sober reflection of selected official judges to weigh the evidence and proffer an opinion. Given our current situation and circumstance, the appointment of judges in this case would be time consuming and unwieldy. In the interests of our Constitutionally guaranteed right to a speedy trial, the recognized leadership of this group has elected to hold a town hall meeting to openly discuss this case and to resolve the matter with a binding vote of the residents of this shelter. The result of the vote will be final and not subject to any appeal.

General McIntyre spoke again. "These circumstances, as I have already stated, are extremely grave. A respected member of our community has, allegedly, proposed a coup; to install himself as the new leader of a new American nation. Customarily the punishment for any act of treason against the President, the Constitution and the nation has been death. This man who stands before you faces that potential penalty. Moreover, his family has been brought into this situation. He has, wittingly or un-, caused the lives of four additional people to be directly affected by the decision of this body."

The general looked at each of the faces gathered before them. "As a society it is our responsibility to listen to the testimony of all involved and to make what could possibly be the most difficult and important decision we have ever been asked to make. The mechanics of this proceeding will be simple: The accusers will present their testimony. The accused will have the opportunity to call any witnesses he may have for his defense and we will complete the proceeding with a statement from the accused directly to you, his jurors."

The President spoke again. "As you might imagine, we are setting a new precedent in law today. The format of the trial will be a blueprint for juris prudence for years to come. Fellow Americans; fellow *survivors*," he said looking meaningfully into their eyes, "today we make a new history. Today we define who this band of Americans will be. And who we will become. This precedent will define the character of our new American nation and will define who we are going to be for generations to come. General Grabowski, please take a seat. This trial will come to order."

Grabowski did as he was told, sitting before the tribunal. He remained stoic but not quite defiant. The only hint that he was perturbed was a thin line of perspiration forming at his hairline and on his upper lip.

"General William Grabowski, you stand accused of treason against the Constitution of the United States of America," stated McIntyre. "Do you wish to say anything before the trial begins?"

"No," replied Grabowski, his voice cracking slightly. He cleared his throat and repeated a bit louder "No. These people have a right to hear everything. Let's please get it over with."

"Very well then. Major Orlando Gomez, please come forward."

Major Gomez rose from his second row seat and stood next to the general. "Orlando Gomez, do you swear to tell the truth, the whole truth and nothing but the truth so help you God?"

"I'm sorry sir, but I no longer believe in God."

McIntyre scowled and gave an exasperated sigh. "Alright, do you swear by all that you hold most dear and sacred that your testimony today will be completely truthful?"

"Yes sir," said Gomez. "I can do that and I do so swear."

"Excellent," said McIntyre. "Please proceed."

Major Gomez stood before the crowd and related his story of General Grabowski's offer—a story that was nearly identical to that of Colonel Wilkes'. His testimony was followed by one Colonel Bair; again identical to Colonel Wilkes'. Finally Colonel Wilkes himself came forward and related the details of his meeting with General Grabowski.

General McIntyre stepped forward again. "Gentlemen, thank you for your testimony. General Grabowski, do you have any witnesses you would like to call on your behalf?"

"No," said Grabowski. "No-one."

"Then do you have a statement you would like to make?"

"Yes," said Grabowski, looking at his hands folded in his lap.

"Please do so," said McIntyre.

General Grabowski stood slowly, collected his thoughts for a moment, took a deep breath and began to speak. "Ladies and gentlemen, everything these officers have told you today is the absolute truth." A murmur coursed throughout the room. "I did plan an attempt to overthrow the power of our President. It was my design to create a new leadership structure for this group of survivors, with me at its head. I don't suppose it is necessary to tell you that I am sorry. And not only sorry because I got caught but *genuinely* sorry—for much more than you can even imagine. If you will permit me, I would like to share a story.

"Many years ago, when I was a young man, I felt an intensely strong bond with my country. So strong that I elected to spend my professional life in its service. I have had the opportunity to see that service at its most challenging; its most dangerous. I have stood on the front lines of combat and faced America's enemies at close range. Along the way I have made many, many personal sacrifices for the betterment of this country and our way of life. With more than my fair share of good fortune I have been rewarded greatly by the system I served.

"Somewhere along the line it seems that I lost sight of my youthful goal. I became convinced that somehow I was more important than the country I served...that I deserved to be powerful, and that I had some kind of right to control everything around me.

"You may find this hard to believe but I was not even aware of this...this person I had become...until just a few hours ago. I'm not talking about when General McIntyre came to my quarters to arrest me. It actually happened after he left. You see, as I was locked in my room I had the opportunity to see myself as others see me. I overheard a conversation of the two young men responsible for guarding me. I have to tell you, their conversation was extraordinary; humbling. Their love for our country; their belief in the values of our Constitution; their *trust* in the men and women who have been granted the responsibility of safekeeping our ideals.... I was reminded of a young man from my own past. A brash, junior officer who believed so strongly in his country that there was no room to suffer fools. I fear that, had I seen then what I was to become, I may have stepped a little closer to the flying bullets when I was in combat. It became unnervingly clear to me who I had become and how deeply I had violated their trust. Your trust.

"I have abused the privileges of my position, but in

one way more than in any other. While you suffered in the knowledge that your loved ones were perishing outside, horribly and painfully, I secretly moved my own family into the protection of this mountain. The President of the United States gave me a direct order that no-one would come into this shelter. In my hubris I felt no need to respect this order and so, being blind to his and all of your suffering, I selfishly brought my dear wife, my daughter and her husband and my son here where I knew they would be safe.

"Ladies and gentlemen, I am guilty of the crime of treason. In your judgment of me I ask no quarter and I expect the most stringent punishment. As a leader I understand the scope of my crime and the necessity of swift, sure reprimand. I will however, ask that you do not include my family in this. To be sure, they do not belong in here with you—their fate was to have been as that of *your* families. But I can assure you that none of them was ever aware that they were part of my criminal behavior. To them, the invitation to join us in this enclave was no more than a stroke of good luck. A happy coincidence.

"So it is that I beg of you, do not include my family in your decision of my punishment. I alone was, and am, responsible. And although I realize how very late it is for this, I want to apologize to each and every one of you for my misdeeds. I am truly sorry."

Grabowski finished speaking with his head bowed, his hands clasped in front of him. He sat down slowly and looked to his wife in the front row. Her face was ashen—she was completely stricken by all that had happened in the past few hours.

"Cookie," he said, eyes pleading, "I am so very sorry. I love you too much and I just couldn't stand the thought of letting you go. Please forgive me?"

She stared back at him in disbelief. Her eyes were wide; she quivered and shook and she was completely horrified.

The President spoke now. "It would appear that we *have* no burden of proof: General Grabowski freely admits that he is guilty of treason. We must now discuss the punishment for his crime. Because this will affect every occupant of this mountain, we will discuss options openly and freely. If you have an opinion in this matter, now is the time to speak—no-one will be denied his or her right to voice their thoughts. I open the floor to discussion at this time."

Colonel Wilkes was the first to speak. "General Grabowski has admitted his guilt—I must say I'm a bit surprised. American law is clear in this situation: The penalty for treason is death. Therefore General Grabowski must be put to death. Our only question is how to do it."

The thoughtful Security Policeman who guarded the door was next to speak. "I agree that the general must be put to death. But we have more to discuss: What are we going to do about his family?"

A woman near the back stood up and said "Gentlemen, I don't believe the situation is decided. In fact, far from it. In case you haven't realized, we are among the very few survivors of a global calamity. To recklessly put anyone to death for the sake of an act of arrogance is ridiculous!"

Ignoring her comments, Colonel Wilkes continued as if thinking aloud. "Now that I think about it, perhaps it would be more appropriate to put his family to death and let him live, suffering in the knowledge that he alone was responsible. That's really the only way that he could suffer as we all have."

Leah Sandon spoke. "Are you people insane? Listen to what that woman is saying! We're talking about killing people—more human beings dying, not because of some tragedy, but because we feel like playing God. General Grabowski has obviously become aware of the gravity of his misdeeds and he appears to be genuinely remorseful. Are we to start killing one another for perceived infractions now? When will the killing stop then?"

General Grabowski's son stood next. "I realize that I have a vested interest in this, but the President said that anyone who has an opinion has the right to speak. Well, I have an opinion. First of all, I can't even believe that this is happening. Christ, Dad, what were you smoking?

"You know, six months ago I would have been all for capital punishment in the case of treason. I've been raised to believe in the United States, in the Constitution, my whole life. You don't mess with that. My father taught me that.

But now: Holy shit! With everything that has happened: Asteroids, earthquakes, volcanoes, tidal waves, nuclear winter—our whole planet's been wiped out. And we're sitting here talking about treason.... And my dad's the one who's guilty of the act!

"So here's what I think: I think that that lady is right. Here we are in a cave and we're talking about exterminating the very individuals we're trying to save. How does that make sense?"

Colonel Wilkes looked coolly at the boy. "Put 'em outside. That's how we'll do it. Let them have a fighting chance, just like my family did. Open the damn door and chuck the whole family out there."

Cookie Grabowski couldn't stand the shock any longer. She wretched out an anguished scream and buried her face in her hands, unable to face the crowd, unwilling to look at her husband.

Mark Zorbas now spoke. "You know, the general makes an interesting point. He is guilty and he must be punished. Traditionally the punishment is death but here we find ourselves in circumstances so far outside of tradition that we have no framework to make an easy decision. Here's some things to think about: The guy's old. So's his wife. Let's say we do chuck them outside. More food for the rest of us. The girl and her husband: They're breeders. We're gonna need kids to repopulate, so they can stay. And the kid can stay too—looks like he's got a strong back. We're gonna need some workers when we get out of this place."

Carmen Fletcher shuddered when he said this. "I don't think it's appropriate that we discuss these people as if they were cuts of meat at the grocery store, Mark."

"Well, like it or not Carmen, it's what they are. It's what we all are. Fuck up, get out. That's what I say."

The discussion continued for another hour. Most, it seemed, were for some sort of punishment short of banishing the family. Those who were for leaving them outside were adamant and vocal. Finally the President called the discussion to a halt. "It seems that we have heard what we need to hear. Unless someone has something further to add which we have not yet heard—in terms of proposed punishment—we will vote on the fate of General Grabowski. Those in favor of casting the General outside, please signify by raising your hand. I'll need a couple of volunteers to count hands in the hallways, please."

The votes were tallied up. "Now those in favor of banishing the general's family." This time a very few hands were raised. "Next, banishing the general with his family...." A similar number of hands went up. "Finally, those in favor of allowing the general and his family to stay unmolested." This time, as with the first vote, a number of volunteers were needed to count the raised hands.

The volunteers brought in their tallies and the votes were recorded. "Ladies and gentlemen," said the President," it would appear that we have a quorum. By a margin of 23 votes, the general and his family will be allowed to stay with us in the mountain." There was a great deal of murmuring and discussion at the announcement.

"Please...Please. First and foremost, I will remind you that the vote is binding and that appeals will not be heard. Second, I will ask that we, as a group, remain civilized with regard to General Grabowski and his family. Regardless the depth of our personal feelings in this matter. Our society has spoken. Personal acts of retribution," he looked directly at Colonel Wilkes, "will not be tolerated." He took a breath and drew himself up to his full height. "Finally, there must be some form of punishment meted out." The President stood before Grabowski and said: "I cannot mete out a punishment that would be fit for your arrogance, general. I can only hope that a gesture will suffice in completing your disgrace. As of this moment, I hereby dishonorably discharge you, Mr. Grabowski, from the service of this nation. You will no longer wear the uniform of the United States' Army. You will forfeit any privileges due to your rank. Your private quarters will be vacated immediately." Then, turning around, he said to the crowd, "This will complete the proceeding. Thank you, ladies and gentlemen, for your participation."

T he trial was over but its effects were only just beginning to be felt. Among those most impacted were the children. Leah sat with Jacob and Rebecca talking quietly while the twins slept in their car seats.

"Momma, I still don't get it," Rebecca was saying. "Some of those people wanted to kill that man. And his family too. Why would they want to do that? Killing is wrong!"

"Well sweetheart, that man committed a crime against America. Against all of us. Do you remember the part where he said that he thought he was more important than everyone else? That was his real crime: Believing that any one person can be more important than all the rest of us."

"Wait a second, Mom," Jacob interjected. "Back in the trial you were defending the guy. Now you're telling us he's guilty. Which one is it?"

"Does he deserve to be killed, Momma? Even though killing is bad?"

Leah sighed a great, long sigh. "Children, this topic involves so very many things. We're talking about the law, we're talking about politics, we're talking about morality, and justice, and compassion, and forgiveness. We have a very complex situation here that involves all of these. And the crazy part is that what is right in one area — let's say the law for example — is completely wrong in another area; like compassion and forgiveness. In this situation we have to balance which is more right."

"What would Dad have said?" asked Rebecca.

"Becca!" said Jacob. "We're not supposed to talk about Dad!"

"No, Jacob," retorted Leah sternly. "Your father was a beautiful man. We will not dishonor his memory by refusing to talk about him." Jacob was stung by the rebuke and looked confused. "My dear children," said Leah, gathering one in each arm, "what your father did was terrible; horrible. But you must understand how he was feeling. Everything your father had ever learned — had ever known — was taken away from him. And there was no way for him to replace that or to deal with it. In a way your father was stuck in a prison, with a very strict set of rules. When the number one rule got broken, he wasn't able to cope. All the rest of the rules no longer applied. I think your father felt that he no longer had a place on this earth so he went to look for his place in Heaven."

Jacob looked skeptical. "Children," said Leah gently but firmly, "we will remember your father with all the love we ever felt for him. We will talk about him. We will remember his hugs, his laughter, his kindness and the special love he felt for all of us. We will not let the memory of that wonderful man perish. Understand?"

They both nodded. Rebecca said "So what would Dad have said about this?"

Leah thought for a moment. "Dad was kind of a contradiction. He loved Jesus more than anything. He followed the commandments very strictly and to the letter. But he loved this country, too. He would have punished anyone very severely if they tried to do anything to harm America. It's difficult for me to predict. I would like to think that he would come down on the side of Jesus and forgiveness but I'm afraid that his strong feelings for this nation may have taken over in this situation. What do you think?"

Jacob piped up, "He would've had the guy fried. You know Dad...."

Rebecca looked thoughtful. "I am going to believe that Daddy would forgive him. He'd be mad — that's just the way he is. But, in the end, he would understand that forgiveness is more important than that man's crime."

"I like that, Becca. I'm going to believe that too," said Leah, giving her a squeeze.

"Momma," said Rebecca.

"Yes, my sweet?"

"Is he going to come?"

"Is who going to come?"

"Is Jesus going to come? Will He come back now like He's supposed to, or will we have to believe something new?"

"Oh, my," said Leah. "Of course, I don't know.... No-one really knows for sure, in spite of how they might talk or what they might say. Your father believed that He would come back. Believed it with all his heart. Do you know, my dears, I think that it is mostly a story. I think that the Jesus story is to teach us all how we are supposed to act in this world. I'm not sure that all of the story is true. I think I believe that we're supposed to understand that Jesus was a model for us all—an example that we're supposed to try to follow. But I don't think that He's going to come back and make everything better for us. I don't think that He's the Savior like the stories tell us. I think that we're *all* supposed to be saviors. Saviors of ourselves...and each other. If Jesus ever returns it will be in the form of the way we treat each other. How much we can love each other, even when we don't feel like it."

"People are calling you the 'Pastor' now, Mom."

"What? Who? Who's calling me a pastor?"

"Everybody. They are all saying that God is in you and He's speaking through you. Do you think that's true? Is

God speaking through you?"

"Well," said Leah, flustered, "I guess God speaks through all of us. Certainly He could be speaking through me...as much as anyone else."

"I like that you're going to be the new Pastor, Momma," said Rebecca. "I think you'll make a really good one."

Leah hugged her children tightly and wondered at all they had said.

Karl Roscoe

Dennis Schweigert and Carmen Fletcher were officially an item. They developed the relationship slowly; she kept busy with her medical work, he occupied himself providing advisories to the leadership group. And explaining many, many times to many, many individuals what had happened and what they might expect from the future. But, after a year had passed in their new home, the work slacked off and they found themselves able to spend more time in each other's company.

As couples are wont to do, they sought out private spaces where they could, at least, feel as if they were alone. During these private times they had the conversations that couples have and got to know one another. Due to the unique nature of their courtship however, their conversations took on a very distinct philosophical bent. They found themselves discussing much more important topics than what color eyes their children might have and where they'd like to settle as a family. After the trial they were having one such discussion.

"Was Mark always so callous?" asked Dennis.

"I guess he always had a bit of that in him back in med school," she replied, "but never to the extent he showed in there."

"So is there some kind of psychological reason for that? Is it just a natural course of events that it would get worse as the years go by?"

"Well, I can't imagine that the stress of having the whole world blow up and being trapped underground with 1,500 strangers is going to improve on any latent tendencies," she answered. "But if you're asking me to psychoanalyze him you're going to need to give me a few years and a whole lot of cooperation from Mark before we'll get any kind of satisfactory answer." Dennis grimaced at her answer.

"You know," she said in a confidential tone, "we were only together for a short time and med school is so intense there's not a lot of time to spend getting to know each other. The intensity of the program wipes you out mentally. Relationships tend to be pretty physical. Not like here..." she said smiling and snuggling closer. He wrapped his arms around her.

After a few moments of quiet, Dennis spoke again.

"That whole trial was something else."

"I guess that's why they call it a trial," she said, trying hard to be contented in his embrace.

He didn't get the hint. "I think the whole idea of the thing was pretty important. You know, some precedents were set here that are going to affect any future society dramatically."

She sighed. It was obvious that he wasn't about to let her just enjoy his company in silence. His words struck a chord with her. "Dennis, how likely is it that we'll have a society in the future? I mean, even ten years from now?"

"Well," he hedged, "you know I'm a geologist, not a biologist. But, as I have done a bit of research on the topic, and I'm the closest thing to an expert on it, I'd say our chances are just this side of fifty-fifty. Getting through the first couple of years is going to look like the easy part compared with what we're going to be facing in the very near future. Right now it's a frozen wasteland out there. The dust is going to hang around for a bit, continuing to block sunlight from reaching the surface. When that dust starts coming out of the atmosphere it'll bring poisons with it, contaminating water supplies. I think that's going to be step number one: Providing a safe, contamination-free water supply.

"Then we'll need something to eat — a source of food. So where's it come from? Do we try to grow it? What plants will be hardy enough to withstand the conditions out there? And how many varieties can be grown so we don't go crazy eating just one type of plant? And where the hell are we going to get the seeds?"

"I'm afraid I'm not a very good vegetarian," Carmen sighed. "What hope do I have of ever eating another steak?"

"Excellent point," said Dennis. "We're omnivores. What's an omnivore to eat when everything is dead? Will cannibalism become a viable option for us?"

"Ick!" she said. "Who said anything about cannibalism? Don't talk like that! It's gross and totally disgusting."

'But based totally on fact!" he said. "Here's what little I can remember from my Anthropology courses: When the Pacific islanders outgrew their island's resources, they would set out to find a new island with more food and assets. Eventually they ran out of islands to move on to. They had to resort to a more, shall we say, 'unconventional' means of food acquisition. The real difference between them and us is that we will be incorporating cannibalism as a conscious decision...solely because the survival of the species is on the line."

"We can't make that kind of decision, Dennis. It's far too horrible!"

"I'm afraid we'll be faced with that conclusion and much worse," he countered.

"Ugh," she shuddered. After a while she spoke again. "So, in keeping with your freshman core courses, I guess we're just going through Maslow's hierarchy of needs here then, right?"

Dennis nodded. "That pretty well nails it. Food, water, shelter...then we need to feel safe from the environment before we can begin to pursue literature, music and the like. Our children's children will look at our experiences here in the mountain as the Golden Age."

"It's a bit premature to be talking about our grandchildren, don't you think?" she chided.

He smiled gently when he answered. "You know Carmen, we are quite literally Adam and Eve. The children in this mountain are, without the slightest exaggeration, the future of the human race. If we were to have children," he gave her a little squeeze, "their destiny would be to be the anchor of humankind. Their names will be famous among their grandchildren the way that our contemporaries can cite names from the bible. Damn," he chuckled, "we'll even be famous, just for surviving!"

"'Dennis the Seer'?" she teased. "Or perhaps 'Carmen the Fertile'?"

"More like 'Dennis the Extremely Lucky'," he laughed, "and 'Carmen the Beautiful and Very, Very Smart'!"

She poked him playfully. She was pleased with the compliment. They sat quietly together for a few minutes. Her face took on a melancholy, wistful look. She was too quiet.

"What...?" he said.

"Oh...," she sighed dejectedly. "Agustin," she answered. "He had children." She shook her head. "They were his future, his present, his everything. Do you think he's with them now?"

"I'd like to think that," he said. "Who knows, Carmen?"

"He was so sad," she said. "I'd read about it in class, of course, but it's impossibly difficult to watch. Who would believe that it's possible to actually die of a broken heart?"

"He died a long time ago, Carmen. You should let him go."

"They told us in med school that we would lose patients — that sometimes people just decide to die without consulting us. I had one patient who committed suicide — a deeply disturbed person — but somehow our loss of Agustin seems more difficult. More personal."

Dennis tried again. "He came to you with the stated intention of ending his own life. You can't let yourself believe you could have changed that. Short of bringing his family back from the dead, what could you have done?"

"I know," she said forlornly. "I know. I just wish it hadn't happened, that's all."

"Let him go," said Dennis, patting her hair. "Let him go."

The sat together in their intimacy and mulled private thoughts.

"Cheyenne, this is Unity—anybody home?" Viktor Kasparof was in the mood for company. The astronauts had fallen into a routine with the Cheyenne survivors. When they were passing overhead and wanted to hear a different voice, they'd call down looking for someone who wanted the same. "How about it, Cheyenne...anyone want to talk?"

Today it was the President who was listening next to the radio. "Go ahead, Unity. Is that you, Viktor?"

"I suppose is difficult to disguise this voice," he replied in his thick accent. "And this is my friend the President?" he asked.

The President laughed. "It would appear I'm spending too much time in this room!"

Kasparof chuckled. "It has been my pleasure to make you as my friend," he said.

"So how are things looking from up there, Viktor?" They had been in the mountain twelve months now and this was always the first question for Unity's crew.

"Dust cover remains heavy. We're getting average surface temperatures between 0 and -20 degrees C. This morning we saw Antarctic coastline again. Perhaps this will not last so long as we had feared...."

"We could only hope," responded the President. "What's the news from the others?"

"We lost contact with Japan few days ago. We're not so worried. They've been having antenna problems since first contact. I expect they are fine. South Africa is not so good. They are having serious food problems. We've been talking up here; no good ideas from us."

"We've been discussing that quite a bit down here as well. I'll have our best thinkers put their brains on it. There must be *some* way to keep them going."

"We feel same," said Kasparof. "My friends in Ukraine were drunk again. I didn't want to speak in that condition. They worry me most."

"I wish there was something we could do to help." said the President.

"I suppose they will make it OK," he said. "Adversity is like wife to us."

"And Argentina?" asked the President.

"Argentina is like you," he answered. "Well prepared, well stocked, ready for long march."

"That much is good to hear." he changed the subject. "Hey, I understand you guys had a close call...."

"Too close!" exclaimed Kasparof. "Fifty meters! Without ground controllers to fly satellites, suddenly they are everywhere up here!"

"Seems like fifty meters isn't *that* bad," said the President.

"My friend," responded Kasparof patiently, "picture you, being in oil can far above planet. Now comes out-of-control, shiny satellite traveling at 2000 kilometers per hour. You watch the shiny get brighter; closer. It looks like it will hit you for sure. You say goodbye to your friends because this is the time you will die. Then: Zoom! Over just like that. Fifty meters is nothing at such speed!"

The President gave a low whistle. "I guess I'm just not accustomed to dealing with things that move so fast. Are there more up there you have to worry about?"

"More, yes. Many more. All out of control. And we never know where to look for them. They just come. Just like that."

"How horrible!" said the President. "How can you sleep with that constant threat?"

"This is why I called today," said Kasparof, his tone changing to one of serious professionalism. "I must speak with you as President of United States and owner of Space

Station."

"OK...I don't really own Unity," he replied. "What do you have in mind?" His curiosity was piqued.

"My crew and I—we have talked. Our supplies are running very low. We are full of garbage. Our station smells like dirty barn. We can't stay here much longer. It becomes too dangerous."

"Where can you go? I mean, there's really not a way out for you, is there?" The President was thinking as he spoke. "Assuming you could get out of the station, you'd have to worry about re-entry. The burn would melt your craft before you ever saw the ground. And even if you survived that, there's the landing to worry about. How and where could you touch down safely? And right now this entire planet is a giant ice cube. How will you live once you make it back to Earth?" The President was firm in his conclusion. "I'm sorry, Viktor but you're talking about a suicide attempt here!"

Kasparof responded slowly, quietly. "And you feel that staying here, slowly starving ourselves of food and oxygen is an alternative which is more acceptable?" There was a heavy silence for a moment. "We have talked much about this plan."

"Plan?" queried the President. You already have a plan?"

"Yes," responded Kasparof. "You can't seriously imagine that we would just sit here and watch pretty world go by.... We have been discussing this for long time now. We have escape vehicle. It has required some modification but we have worked on it and it will suit our needs. All will be ready for our attempt in one, maybe two weeks."

"One or two weeks..." stammered the President. "But that's not nearly long enough!"

"Enough for who, my friend? You in your comfortable little rabbit hole or us having missiles flying past each day? Would you have us die slowly up here so that you might feel better about your conscience? Or die in a brilliant flash across the skies, as we have tried to live our lives?"

"But Viktor, you're my *friend*. I don't know if I can let you..."

"Then decide as your nation's leader," said Kasparof, cutting him off. "Decide in favor of the honor of the men who still serve. Do you believe we will not disobey you?" There was no mistaking the meaning of the question.

"I...I...."

"My friend," continued Kasparof, "we have stayed this long to honor you. The ground survivors—you needed link to each other. We have been that link—so that you know you are not alone. But our time grows too short." Kasparof was straightforward. "We will not die in space. We will die trying to return to our beloved home. From you, Mr. President, we are asking blessing for our last mission. And from my friend..." he continued, "...I ask understanding that this is way I have lived my whole life. Better that it ends this way too."

Realizing his position and total lack of other options, the President sat up straight in his chair. "Commander Kasparof, in the name of the United States' government, I authorize you to take whatever steps you deem necessary to save the lives of your crew."

"Thank you, Mr. President. We will give more details for our plan. But now that we have your understanding it will be much easier. My crew are smiling now. Much relieved."

"I will smile too, Viktor," he answered, "when my friend returns home from his brave and dangerous journey."

A gain the gathering hall was full of people. The President had called for a town hall meeting. He had said only that he had an important announcement and that the survivors had some decisions to make.

Even after a year underground, he was still accustomed to making entrances. He strode to the center of the room and faced the expectant crowd. "Ladies and gentlemen," he began, "our astronauts aboard the space station Unity are preparing to embark on the most dangerous mission ever attempted. Their food and water supplies are running desperately short. The air inside the station has become so stale that it is barely breathable.

"Despite these circumstances, our brave crew has elected to stay aboard as long as possible in order to provide a liaison between our group and the other survivors scattered around the earth. However, due to the circumstances aboard the station, it is no longer practical for them to do this for our benefit.

"Yesterday I spoke with Commander Kasparof. He asked for my permission to abandon the station and attempt to return to the earth. The escape craft they plan to use is serviceable, though it will require some modification for this journey. I am told that the heat shield is adequate for re-entry and the parachute system has repeatedly tested well.

"After much discussion among themselves, they have chosen to attempt a hard touchdown on land, as there exists no sea rescue capability. Their most favorable landing site is the Great Plains of North America. Their calculations are rudimentary at this time but they'll be attempting a landing in eastern Colorado...a safe distance from the Rocky Mountains and still close enough for an attempt at land travel to this enclave.

"I suppose that it goes without saying that this mission has extremely high probability *against* its success. The three crewmembers are completely prepared. They have consistently faced impossible odds and have each made a career out of beating those odds. I can think of no more capable a group of people to make such an effort.

"I'd like to request that those of you who are in close contact with Unity's crew offer words of encouragement in the coming week. It is absolutely imperative that they feel the full weight of our support. They will embark on their journey next week. Godspeed to them in their endeavor."

A general murmur of agreement went through the crowd. "And now," continued the President, "our next order of business. The laws written for this nation; the backbone of this country, our Constitution, may no longer apply to this group in our current situation. I believe that the time is right to address the framework for the future of our people."

The crowd stirred, registering disapproving looks and sounds. He held his hands up in a 'stop' gesture and said "Wait, please; listen. I am not suggesting that we abandon the Constitution altogether. Merely that we study out present condition and make some reasonable guesses as to what the future may hold. Armed with that knowledge, we could modify the existing document to fit our situation. I'm looking for a group who may be interested in studying the Constitution and who will propose some well-thought-out modifications to carry our offspring into a successful future. Virtually anyone can offer input to the study group and any changes will be subject to ratification by a majority of us — democracy will remain our foundation.

A man spoke out. "I'm getting a little tired of you coming around and telling us what to do. I didn't vote for you and, considering the circumstances, I know for sure nobody in this room elected you *President*. I think maybe it's time to reevaluate our leadership."

Another man chimed in. "I sure as hell didn't vote

for you!"

"Gentlemen," said the President. "Ladies and gentlemen, surely this is not the appropriate time for politics!"

"I vote for General Mac," said the first.

"Very well," conceded the President, "in the absence of a Congressional body, I will institute the impeachment process immediately. Again we'll use a simple majority vote and the result will be binding. As there is currently no sitting Vice President; elected or un-," he said with a pointed look at the upstart, "we will all be subject to martial law, with General McIntyre as our acknowledged leader, in the event of successful impeachment proceedings."

Mac stood from where he was sitting and said, "Now hold on, Mr. President. We just went through all this business not very long ago. I'm pretty sure we all concluded we're happy with our leadership the way it is...."

"Mac," said the President, "as you well know, very often the best way to deal with an issue is to tackle it head-on. If our two discontented citizens are unhappy enough to speak up in this gathering, you can be certain there are others thinking along similar lines." Speaking to the crowd again, he said, "Let's avoid all the sniping and bad feelings and get this out in the open and settled."

McIntyre was adamant. "Mr. President, I think the exercise is foolish. And wasteful of our time. I'm certainly not bucking for any more responsibility than I've already got."

Mac, these people deserve an immediate answer. If the result is my lawful impeachment then we have to have some sort of succession in place. I'd rather not have to order your cooperation...."

"Well," he conceded, "if it makes our lives here just a little easier, I suppose it I can suffer a bit of bullshit."

"Excellent," said the President. "Now, with regard to my fitness to continue to serve as your President, a motion has been brought forward and has been seconded. All in favor of impeaching the sitting President of the United States, signify by a show of hands."

About thirty hands went in the air as a woman said, "Oh, this is ridiculous!"

"All opposed?" asked the President. Every other hand in the facility was raised. "The 'nay's' carry the vote; motion fails. Now:" he said, "Are there any other concerns you would like to have addressed in this forum?" No one spoke. "Well then," he continued, "I'll be needing some volunteers for a study committee."

Karl Roscoe

When the tumbling and banging finally stopped, Antonio DiGiammo looked around him. Narita was immediately across the escape pod. His mouth was open and his eyes were wide, staring at DiGiammo. To his left he saw Kasparof slumped over in his seat. Kasparof's right arm looked mangled. At the very least his wrist was shattered. "Guess we made it, Phil. Can you believe it?"

Narita made no answer. He continued to stare, openmouthed at DiGiammo.

"Phil? Did you hear me? Are you OK?"

Still no answer. In fact, there was no movement at all from him. His eyes stared blindly forward, unblinking. He didn't appear to even be breathing. Then DiGiammo noticed the jagged shard of metal beneath Narita's right armpit.

There was a small red blotch staining the opposite side of his space suit.

"Merda!" said DiGiammo. That wasn't in the plan. He took a few moments to do a quick visual scan of his own body, just in case. All the parts appeared to be there and in working order. He decided to unbuckle and see how badly Kasparof was hurt. As he was trying to negotiate the clasp he heard a groan come from the station commander. "I'm coming, Viktor. Just try to lie still." He got the stubborn clasp undone and fell out of his seat, almost on top of Kasparof. Gravity had returned. He struggled against his own weight, trying to sit up enough to unbuckle Kasparof.

The commander was conscious now, smiling thickly through his pain. "We'll have some story for friends in Cheyenne, eh Antonio?"

"Some story, Viktor," DiGiammo agreed. "Let me get you out of this strap. Move to the left, can you?"

Kasparof shifted slightly, then cried out in pain. "What did you do to my arm? I thought you were good pilot!" There was the shadow of a smile behind the wincing, strained face. He was doing his best to keep his spirits up through the throbbing in his right wrist.

"Good enough to get you here alive!" snapped DiGiammo. "Now help me get you out of your seat."

"Ask Phil," said Kasparof. "Two will work better than one."

"Narita is gone," answered DiGiammo, keeping busy

with the belt buckle. "He didn't survive the landing."

"So. There's one who can complain."

"*Idiota!*" DiGiammo was unnerved by Narita's death and wanted to get away from their deceased companion as quickly as possible. "If you don't help me, then I will just leave you here in this wreck of a space ship!"

"OK, OK," groused Kasparof through gritted teeth. He shifted as far left as his strength would let him.

"Got it!" said DiGiammo triumphantly as Kasparof slid to the floor.

"You're sure he's dead?" queried Kasparof.

"You tell me," replied DiGiammo with a nose in Narita's direction.

Kasparof noted the blank stare, the absolute stillness and the metal shard piercing the spacesuit. "We may yet call him lucky one. Is big job we have now."

Rather than responding, DiGiammo began crawling around the cramped inside of their escape vehicle. It was extremely banged up from the landing. Neatly stored survival items had been strewn all around. He located the first aid kit and spun on his knees to face Kasparof again.

"You don't like to talk about death, eh Antonio?"

DiGiammo crossed himself quickly. "Let me see your hand," he said.

While the Italian worked swiftly in splinting and bandaging the crushed wrist, Kasparof kept up an unwelcome running commentary. "So, we survive in America, while American does not. Ironic, nyet? I was getting beaten too much up to get a good fix on our landing zone. Perhaps we lost one parachute.... Perhaps we lost two. How far from Cheyenne are we now? How deep is ash outside? How long will food supply last for two instead of three? Many questions, my friend."

"One thing at a time, Viktor. First we get your arm ready for travel. Then we collect our equipment and prepare ourselves for the same."

"And our friend, Narita: Do we bury him and say nice words over grave?"

DiGiammo tightened the last knot on the splint just a bit too much. Kasparof winced. "We do what we need to do to survive, Viktor. We'll rest here for a few hours and then try to navigate to Colorado Springs."

"Rest I suppose is good. Colorado Springs could be very far away. Could be very difficult to reach. I will enjoy some rest before big journey."

The two men did their best to find a comfortable position in the tiny craft where they did not have to look at Phillip Narita's blank, pale face, still staring at DiGiammo's empty seat.

They had been underground for thirteen months. It was time. Today was the day Dr. Mark Zorbas would win Alexis Coffey's hand. He knew it. He felt it in his bones. He had spent months doing the groundwork for this day. He had rehearsed his actions, his lines—everything would be perfect.

Today, after Alexis finished sitting for hours by the door, she would retreat to a storeroom deep in the back of the mountain. There she would close and lock the door and sit in total isolation until the evening gathering for dinner had broken into a few scattered diners. Then she would eat alone, as she always did, and retire to leaf through her faded, worn magazines.

Mark was well-prepared. Today would be different

for her. He had been to the storeroom. He had stocked it with the items he needed to make this evening a success. A bottle of wine he'll liberated from General McIntyre's office, a package of smoked salmon he'd been hiding all these months, a sentimental Hallmark card with only a few erasure marks and a pair of comfortable blankets upon which they would consummate their newfound love.

Not wanting to appear too eager, he took up a post far down the hall from her room. Despite his wish to be poised and tranquil, he couldn't stop himself from showing up two hours prior to her scheduled arrival. This additional wait caused his stress to be at fever pitch when she finally rounded the corner and opened the door.

Mark was beside himself with the thrill of what was about to happen. He could hardly contain his trembling as he approached the door. He watched his palsied hand reach for the door, then stop and, with a renewed burst of confidence, push against the flat of the door just above the handle. As he knew it would, the door swung inward, smoothly, silently. He stepped boldly into the small room, seeing her sitting on the floor: Legs folded beneath her, leaning against a lower shelf with her chin resting on top of her hands.

She started when she saw movement out of the corner of her eye and immediately barked at him. "This is a private space! Get the hell out of here!" Her eyes darted toward the door handle to confirm that she had locked it. Mark smiled and slowly stripped away the tape he'd placed along the side of the door where it had kept the latch from its intended purpose. He saw anger flash across her eyes as he pushed the door closed.

"I'm Mark," he said, still smiling. "We've met once already."

"I don't give a shit who you are. Get out of here and leave me alone!" Mark's smile never dimmed. He anticipated the outburst. It was completely expected. He had rehearsed this moment many, many times. She would need a firm hand and steady guidance to shepherd her through to her new identity — as Mark Zorbas' woman.

Assuming complete command, he walked to the shelf with the blankets and took them down. Launching into his practiced explanation of how they were meant to be together, that fortune had created the circumstance to seal their bond, he unfolded the blankets and arranged them on the floor. Then he pulled out the wine, uncorked it and poured two coffee mugs half full. Bringing out the salmon, he watched her expression flicker through many shades of disbelief. His hand brushed against hers when he placed the greeting card before her with a witty comment and a flourish. He was too involved in his presentation and his own version of the moment to recognize that she was recoiling in horror and disgust from his touch. He was just a little confused when, at the big finish, she looked at him with unconcealed revulsion; not at all the wonder and admiration he'd imagined. She was supposed to have been convinced beyond all question that he was, unarguably, her soulmate.

Pressing to close the sale, he soldiered on. He was trying hard to ignore her withering glare. "You know it's meant to be, Alex. It's all us from here on out." He waited for the inevitable transformation to take place—for the recognition that his was the superior logic. She simply had no choice but to love him. But it never came. Her face morphed from disgust to bitter mocking.

"You've just got to be shitting me," she jeered. "This is what you've come up with? After a full year underground, this is the best you can do? Let me just clue you in, Jasper—"

"Mark," he corrected.

"Asshole!" she countered. Standing up, she walked past him to the still-open door. Pointing down the hallway outside, she said loudly, "There are literally tens of thousands of people on the other side of that big-ass door out there. People who are desperate to know what I'm wearing and eating. Whose handbag I'm toting. Who I've been partying with. They've been without me for a over year now and they're getting damned anxious about the whole thing. Don't think for even one split second that my being held prisoner in this lame hole in the ground is going to affect my judgment. I decide who I will and won't be seen with. Clue number one: It isn't you!"

Mark was prepared for a bit of disbelief. He predicted that it would take some explanation and discussion to bring her around to his way of thinking but the intensity of her denial took him by surprise. "Look, Alex," he began.

"*Alexis*!" she shouted. "My name is fucking **'Alexis.'** Don't call me Alex, you piece of shit!"

Stung, he tried again. "OK, *Alexis* then. It's us, baby. We were meant to be together." He spread his arms wide, smiled big and said "This is your future, honey!"

She choked out a bitter laugh. "I think I'd rather be dead than stuck with your sorry ass."

Anger flared inside him and he growled through clenched teeth, "That could be arranged...." With a bit of effort he visibly softened and picked up one of the mugs of wine. Reclining on the blanket he tried one more time. He patted the ground next to him and said, "Come on, Alex— *Alexis*. Sit with me here and let's have a drink together. I'm certain you'll fall for me when you give me an opportunity." He smiled his most disarming smile. "I'm actually a pretty terrific guy!"

She spoke slowly, directly, forcefully. "Now get this through your thick skull: This is my personal time and my personal space." With one hand on her hip, she pointed an accusing finger at him. "You and your little picnic are a complete and total invasion of my solitude. Pack up your stuff and get the hell out." She switched hands and pointed at the door. "And I mean now."

Mark stood as well. Ire was quickly growing into full-blown rage. He made one last effort at control. "Sweetheart, you're not giving me a chance...."

"Fuck you, asshole! Get OUT!!"

Blinded now with white hot fury, he smashed the coffee mug against the floor. "BITCH!" he thundered. Reaching back for a full swing, he slapped her hard across the side of her head.

Stunned, but as angry as he was, she raked her nails across his face. "I'll never be with you!" she shouted.

Grabbing a handful of hair in back of her head, he spun quickly, dragging her body along. With the full weight of his body he plowed her face into the shelves. He pulled her back, now-bloodied and, still holding her hair, he slapped her repeatedly. Then he pushed her to the floor where she covered her bleeding face with her hands and glowered viciously at him. He reached behind him to close the door. Her lips began to swell from the battering. She felt at least one broken tooth in her mouth.

Hatred turned to fear as he unbuckled his belt and slid it out of its loops. Slowly, methodically, cruelly, he began to flog her with the hard leather strap. In between whips he would kick her in the ribs, the legs, the head—any exposed body part became a target. Bones cracked. Skin was flayed from the snapping of the belt. When she had been reduced to a whimpering, bloodied heap on the floor, his eyes took on a new, even harder glint. He reached down and unfastened her pants and roughly pulled them as far off from her as he could get them. She was beyond resistance. She was barely conscious of what was happening to her now.

Then he smiled a cold, smug, self-satisfied smile and fumbled with the button on his own pants. One way or another, she would be his.

Karl Roscoe

Carmen was asleep and Dennis Schweigert wanted somebody to talk to. He wandered through the dim hallways for a time, eventually finding himself sitting at one of the empty tables in the galley. He let his mind wander among the thoughts that had been disturbing him. Furrowing his brow, he began to contemplate the future. His meditations were interrupted by a voice, parting the silence like a stone plunking into a still pond.

"Guess I'm not the only one who can't sleep tonight." General McIntyre approached and Dennis motioned for him to sit down.

"Tortured by dreams of the future, I guess. What about you? How come you aren't in bed, Mac?"

"Wrestling with demons, or something. And, at least

for tonight, they're winning."

Dennis chuckled. "I'm afraid that puts me in the loser's circle, too. Can I offer you a coffee? It's old and cold but it'll give you something to hang on to while we wrestle with the bad guys...."

"Pass," said the general with a good-natured laugh. "Goddamn tyrants in charge of this place won't let us make a fresh pot!"

Dennis laughed too. "Well, rationing all our supplies is the only logical approach," he said. "I don't know about you but I'm still in this for the long haul."

"To tell you the truth, that's the very demon I've been locking horns with tonight. We've been in this bunker for a year now, Dennis. It's getting dirty and it smells like old socks." McIntyre crossed his legs and leaned back in his seat. He stretched his arm across the table and drummed his fingers on the surface. "The food and water are likely to last us another year. All in all, we're in a pretty good place physically. But I have to wonder about our resolve. What do you think about our little band of holdouts here?"

"I'm not sure I understand your question, Mac. Are you asking if we have the will to last another year underground? That'd be an unqualified 'yes.' If you're asking if we've all had enough of this place and are ready to move out and on with life, that'd be a 'yes' also. Where do you want to go with this?"

"I wish I knew," he sighed. "Dennis," he said,

changing the subject, "have you ever been in charge of anything?" He stopped drumming his fingers and leaned a tired head into his hand.

"Classrooms, I guess. Why?"

"Hm. For the last year the President and I have been responsible to get 1,486 people from the end of the world to a new beginning of a new world. We've lost twelve so far to injury, disease and stupid shit. I take those losses very, very personally." He looked into infinity as he said this, talking more to himself than to Dennis. "As a leader, I have to trust that my decisions are the absolute best I can make. Every single one of them counts. The most trivial decisions that I make, almost as an afterthought, could have the power to haunt me for the rest of my life. I have the capacity to screw this up so badly that our entire species could end up being wiped out by a single, stupid, thoughtless action. Making a pot of coffee tonight could potentially eradicate the human race!"

"Easy, Mac," soothed Dennis. "It's a little difficult to imagine that one pot of coffee will wipe humanity off the face of the planet. Look at what you've done so far: Almost 1,500 people safely tucked away here, protected from what amounts to a bona fide hell outside." He became a bit more animated as he spoke. Ticking the items off on his fingers, he said, "A power struggle averted with no negative consequence. A guaranteed year of continued comfort and survival, giving us a fighting chance for the future. You've already accomplished more than any other man in history!"

"Thank you, Dennis. I honestly appreciate the sentiment. I guess I just need to let off a little steam. You probably have no clue what kind of pressure I'm feeling."

"Well, let's see: One man, responsible for the survival of the human race—beholden to a small but extraordinarily important band of survivors of a global calamity; accountable for their physical, psychological and social needs; to keep to a set of codes and laws that may no longer apply— OK, I never really thought about it, but your job pretty much sucks!"

"Thanks," returned the general with a hearty laugh. "Thanks a lot!" The two men were silent for a few moments. "It's damned hard, Dennis. Nobody has ever had to lead in such impossible circumstances. Where's the book to tell me about the pitfalls?"

Dennis shook his head and shrugged slightly.

"Yeah," nodded McIntyre. "I'm having to write it day by day. What happens when I screw up? Do you realize it could be years before anyone figures that out? And by then it'll be far to late to correct a bad decision.... Man, I just wish I could shed some of this pressure. If only for a single day."

Dennis thought for a moment before answering. "You didn't ask for this job, did you?"

"Hell no!"

"And is there any way that anyone could have seen this coming?"

"Hell no-..." responded the general, slowing as he spoke. "God damn," he cursed. "I'll be God damned. If any other schmoe on the planet had asked me that question, I'd have had to say no. But you asked me, Dennis. You asked me and the answer is 'yes.' Only one man foresaw it and that man was you."

"Aw, crap!" said Dennis. "That wasn't what I meant." He grew agitated. "Listen, that's *not* what I meant! You know I'm just trying to make a point here...."

"Sorry, boy. Believe it or not, your theories are the reason we're all alive today. How's that for irony?"

Irony," snorted Dennis. "I don't like it. Not even one little bit."

"Maybe you *do* have some better understanding of my position," mused McIntyre. "You've been fighting this fight for a whole lot of years...."

"That's not the fight I've been fighting. At least, I didn't use to think that. Theory is one thing, Mac. To watch your theories unfold—in living color.... I mean, the worst of the worst of my predictions coming true? Compounded by a factor of twenty?! All this has me so scared that all I can do is hide behind a veil of academia. I saw it coming, Mac. Or at least some of it. I swear I could have done more to save more people. So many have died because I failed."

"'Failed' my ass!" rumbled McIntyre. "You warned us all! You were willing to sacrifice everything: Your career, your reputation, your life...just to keep warning us. Hell, you warned us all long past the point that we were no longer interested in listening. It can't possibly be your fault that the establishment—that *we*—chose to ignore you. You did all that you could. And then some. Take solace in this: Because of you, we had a plan in place to populate this mountain. No-one took it as seriously as they should have, or kept the plan up to date but, without that plan, we all would have perished. Everyone."

"Yeah," said Dennis disconsolately. "Yeah." They sat quietly again, each lost in his own thoughts. The general mumbled something about changing his mind and stood up to get a cup of the cold coffee. When he sat back down, Dennis broached a new topic. "You have any idea how we're going to survive out there, Mac?"

"I've been kicking it around some. Tell me again what we can expect to see when we open that door?"

"You understand that this is speculation; that there isn't any real way to predict the course of events based on our reading of the geologic record...."

"Blah, blah, blah. Cut the crap, Dennis. It's impossible to predict. I get it."

"Sorry, Mac. It's just that geologists deal with some pretty hefty time scales. Converting what I know into a period of mere years or even decades.... And then turning that into a prediction that we're all going to wager our lives on—I'm a little out of my league here."

McIntyre nodded. "It's OK, son. Like I said, we're

writing this book day by day. What we do when we get out there is going to be directly related to the conditions we encounter. I need *something* to give me a starting place.

"Alright..." said Dennis, taking a deep breath. "First and foremost, I don't think we should even consider leaving here for at least another year. I figure it's cold out there still. **Really** cold. Best case, I'm thinking the sun's going to finally start penetrating all that atmospheric crap in the next six months or so. The warm-up will be rapid but that's a geologic 'rapid.' Right now it's probably about 20 below, Fahrenheit—not something we want to monkey around with. We're heading into summer. That means a warm-up of about 50 degrees Fahrenheit. That'll get us up to a balmy 30 degrees for this summer. With fall and winter coming on, temperatures will be pretty unbearable. Not unsurvivable but why mess with it when we can stay here in relative comfort?"

"OK, stay here for another year. That's pretty much a given. Then what?"

"Well, that's where it gets fuzzy. Like I said, the geologic record tells us that we can expect warming. I can't tell you that it'll take two years or ten years or even a hundred. I *can* tell you that over time it is going to get hellaciously hot. Then we'll be looking for shelter underground again. Probably for a permanent arrangement. But that only addresses shelter, Mac. I've been killing myself trying to figure out how we're going to eat. And the water purification issue is equally thorny. I mean, we have fifteen hundred people who will need a lifetime of drinking water. Where is that supposed to come from?"

"You actually don't need to worry about that," countered McIntyre. "When we first holed up in here, and had pretty much full access to the internet, I had some people research that very question. I believe that with a lot of luck and a good chemical stash, we can keep a fairly constant supply of fresh water. Food is likely going to be the real issue."

"Carmen and I have had this conversation a few times. I think that seeds are the answer. If you think about it, all that volcanic ash out there, at least when it's mixed with local dirt, is about as fertile a soil as you can get. We just have to find out which crops are going to grow best in it. We can clear a few acre-size plots and till that ash into the soil. It'll be a real job just digging down to ground level but it can be done. We'll have to use our water supply to irrigate it — the sulfides in the natural water will fry anything we try to grow unprotected."

"That's a great idea for the long run. We're going to have to rediscover our agrarian roots. But we have short-term needs as well. What do you propose we eat till we can begin growing food?"

"Mormons," answered Dennis matter-of-factly.

McIntyre was unable to suppress a belly laugh. "Mormons?!" he roared. "We're going to eat Mormons?"

Dennis flushed red. The idea had blossomed fully inside his head and he'd overlooked the fact that he would have to explain his complete line of reasoning. "No, Mac, I don't think we're going to have to eat anyone." He was angry at himself and frustrated with his inability to explain his wondrous idea on the first try. He started over, spelling it out slowly and patiently. "At least, not right away. Listen, Mormons have a year to two-year's supply of non-perishable food stashed in their basements. That's going to be a goldmine for us. We find the temple, dig it out, look for the addresses of the congregants and start checking basements. All the grocery stores will have been sacked. Distribution centers and warehouses will have been looted next. I think cellars and pantries are going to be what carries us through."

General McIntyre was impressed. "I'll be damned. That's pretty close to a brilliant idea. And it beats eating 'em," he chuckled, unable to resist one more jab. "But we're going to have to find one helluva lot of Mormons to feed this crew until we've got some corn and beans in the ground."

"Nobody ever said that any of this was going to be easy, Mac. We're going to be hand-to-mouth for a lot of years."

McIntyre took a swig of cold coffee. "Hmm.... I'm going to have to talk to a few people. Seems that there's more to-" He was interrupted by a squeak, like a sneaker on a gymnasium floor. "Did you hear something?"

"Came from the hallway, I think," said Dennis, turning toward the noise.

A low moan came from the darkness, followed by a

raspy whisper. "Help...." They both leapt to their feet and searched for the source. Not far down the hallway they found a bleeding, bruised, half-naked woman on the floor. A smeared trail of blood led away into the dimness of the hall.

"Oh my God!" gasped Dennis. He stood staring, immobilized.

General McIntyre was a bit more composed and sympathetic. He crouched low to peer at her broken face. "What happened, honey?"

Her eyes, swollen almost shut in the midst of the bruised and disfigured remnants of her face, pleaded silently with him. More whimpering was the only sound she was capable of making.

"We need to get you to the doctor. Give me a hand here, Dennis."

Alexis Coffey' eyes widened with terror and she clutched and clawed at Mac's shirt. "**NO!**" she screeched with her last ounce of strength. Sobbing and sinking to the floor she rasped with her failing voice. "No doctor! No doctor. No doctor...."

Dennis gaped at McIntyre in wonder. "What the hell is going on here, Mac?"

Carmen Fletcher had been awakened by a near-frantic Dennis. He'd attempted to fill her in on the situation but all she got out of the jabbering was that someone had been hurt badly and that Dr. Zorbas was not available to help tonight. With Dennis trotting puppy-like by her side, she marched purposefully through the deserted hallways.

"We were discussing the food problem and how we thought we could solve it when we heard her groan."

"Heard *who* groan? Who am I looking at?"

"Alexis," said Dennis. "Looks like she got the shit beat out of her."

"And tell me again why Mark isn't handling this?"

"Because she freaked, Carmen! I don't think I've

ever seen anyone so scared. She didn't have the strength to do anything but moan but, when Mac said we'd get her a doctor, she started shouting and screaming at us. It was weird!"

Carmen didn't like the sound of any of this. Who had beaten Alexis and why? (Though she had to admit that everyone in the place had at least imagined beating on her at least once....) Why the violent reaction to the offer of help from their only doctor? There was something more to this that needed to be addressed. For now though, she'd have to take things on issue at a time.

A few people had been awakened by the commotion and were standing around Alexis in a small circle. She lay motionless on the floor, curled in a tight ball. Someone had gotten some blankets and she was laying on one and covered by another. Carmen was appalled at the sight of the punished creature that lay before her. Her face was a clotted mass of red and purple. At least one tooth was broken but it was impossible to evaluate further due to her puffy, split, bleeding lips. She held one arm tightly to and underneath her body, hidden by the blanket. The other was visible and told the whole story. Her forearm had received the brunt of the abuse. It was striped with welts and small cuts. The heel of her palm was bruised badly and, although she couldn't see the nails which Alexis had curled tightly into her palms, Carmen knew she would find skin and blood beneath them. Classic defensive wounds. She felt a sickening pitching in her gut. This woman was the very picture of a battering victim.

During her undergrad studies, Carmen had volunteered at a women's shelter. For two years she had seen women come into the house looking exactly like this. Merely being exposed to the kind of cruelty one human being can inflict upon another brought back waves of the horror she used to feel every week at the shelter. Someone had found a reason to beat Alexis to the edge of death. But who? No time for that now. There was healing to be done.

The crowd parted to let Carmen get close to Alexis. She knelt next to the young woman. Her breathing was labored and whistling slightly. Possible rib fractures Carmen noted. "Alexis? Alexis, honey, can you look at me?"

Thin slits appeared in the purple puffs that passed for eyelids. She managed a muffled groan.

"Alexis, we need to get you cleaned up. Then I have to look at you, to see what kind of treatment you need. Will you let me do that?"

She whimpered, then nodded slightly. "OK," she managed to croak.

Carmen directed two of the bystanders to go to the infirmary for a stretcher. They departed at a run and were back in less than five minutes. By now more people were awake and milling about. There was much discussion and speculation about who could have committed this atrocity. Carmen directed her helpers to place Alexis carefully on the stretcher. Twice she cried out in pain but she didn't resist.

Walking behind the crowd of curious onlookers on the way to the infirmary, Carmen spoke quietly with Dennis and General McIntyre. "This woman was beaten by a man. By a vicious man with some pretty major insecurities. I'm sorry to say that I've seen this more than once, both in my studies and in my practice." She shook her head in disgust and then continued. "Tell me exactly what she said to you when she spoke."

Dennis answered first. "She didn't really speak. She was just moaning a lot and then she freaked out and started screaming at us."

"Mac?" inquired Carmen.

McIntyre was thoughtful. "Dennis is right. We were having our discussion in the quiet of the night when we both heard a sound. She was calling for help but she had so little strength we barely heard her. Even as close as she was."

"There's something more," continued Carmen. "What was it you said that brought on the strong reaction?"

"That's been bugging me, quite frankly," said McIntyre. "All I said was 'We need to get you to the doc.' She actually started screaming at that point. 'NO DOCTOR!' Then she ran out of steam completely and just collapsed. Why the Christ wouldn't she want a doctor when she so obviously needs one?"

"Could she have done this to herself?" interrupted Dennis. "Do you think she's finally accepted that there are no fans waiting out there for her and she decided to end it for herself? Another Caleb?" he theorized.

Carmen was grim faced. "No, I don't think that's it. It was definitely a man that did this. Did anyone try to figure out where she came from?"

"As a matter of fact, I sent someone to follow the bloodstains when Dennis was fetching you. She was in a small storeroom. Blood everywhere." Mac furrowed his brow. "It actually looked like a date gone bad, to tell you the truth."

"What do you mean?" demanded Carmen sharply.

"Well, there was a broken bottle of something, a couple of shattered mugs on the floor and some blankets. Whoever it was had been getting cozy with her apparently."

Carmen looked hard at them both. "Have either of you seen Alexis with anyone? Not that I pay close attention or anything, but she's been a loner since the day she got here."

Mac said "I can't say that I keep track of individuals—not even the famous ones. Maybe she did meet someone she thought she might like."

"Ditto," said Dennis. "Pretty much all my time is spent thinking about someone else." He gave a small smile which was returned, only briefly, by Carmen. "Who keeps up with her?" he asked.

"Palmer," said Carmen. "The President's man, Palmer. He keeps pretty close tabs on where she goes and what she does. We should start with him." They all stopped in the hallway. "We're here," she said. "I've got a night's work ahead of me, I'm afraid." She turned to the general. "Mac, I'm going to be looking for signs of rape here and, to be honest, I expect to find them. Whoever did this is a bad, bad guy. You're going to want to find him pronto."

"I've already started the SP's on it. We'll find him, Carmen. This place isn't big enough to hide in."

Carmen entered the infirmary and Dennis and the general walked quietly away.

Mark Zorbas stood over a barely conscious Alexis Coffey and said matter-of-factly, "I guess we've settled that, now." He walked to the door and, with his hand on the handle, said "I won't be calling you." Then, as if to underscore his intent, he added, "*Alex.*" Then he pulled open the door and strode out of the small room. Though he appeared to be calm, his mind was racing. He had no doubt that he would be leaving the mountain and soon. The puzzling aspect was how to get from here to there with as little drama and interaction with the other residents as possible.

His first stop on the way out was the infirmary. There were medications and bandages he would need. There was no way of knowing what he would encounter out there and he wanted to be prepared for any eventuality. Having filled a small bag with everything he could imagine needing, he headed straight for the galley.

In the kitchen he liberated as many MRE's as he felt he could carry. Since there would be nothing to eat on the outside, he'd want as much ready-made food as he could manage. There was a moment—a close call—when he'd heard voices. Schweigert and that irksome general were having some deep conversation out in the dining area. Not wanting to risk discovery, he left almost a third of the MRE's that he'd planned to take with him. Then he slipped quietly out another door.

His next stop was his own quarters. There he could pick up the few things that he considered his own. Then it was on to the supply closet. He was going to need warm clothing for the outside. There was a stock of jackets, wool pants and socks, hats and mittens and military-style cold weather boots. He took what he could wear and placed that and his other items in a backpack that was laying nearby.

Finally he was ready. If things could just stay quiet long enough for him to get to the reservoirs, this thing might just work. As he was slipping around the last corner before the hallway that led to the reservoirs he heard people talking—searching apparently. He supposed they'd found her. Damn! He'd hoped for at least a day's lead on them.

With a face as hard as the heart that beat in his chest, he stole quietly down the dark hallway to his chosen refuge.

E dison Palmer awoke to a general clamor and hubub. People were apparently roaming the hall looking for something and had stopped at his sleeping space. When he opened his eyes people began demanding "Where were you last night?"

His brain was still fogged. "What? Last night? I don't know...why are you people all here?"

A particularly aggressive and large man got right in his face. "What did you do to her, you son of a bitch?"

Coming fully awake, Mr. Palmer sat up to face the man directly. "Thanks for the wakeup call, sport. Now, if you just tell me what you're all worked up about, perhaps we can sort this out."

"You know exactly what we're talking about!"

shouted a woman in the back of the throng. "What did you do to Alexis?"

"Alexis...?" Fear stabbed in the pit of Mr. Palmer's stomach. "Alexis? What's happened to her? Is she hurt?"

"You know better than the rest of us," growled the big man, gripping the front of his shirt tightly.

Mr. Palmer tried unsuccessfully to swipe away the fists holding the material. "What is going on?" he insisted. What's happened to Alexis?"

"Hands off, buddy," said a voice. A Security Policeman pushed through the crowd to separate the two men. His partner hung back at a small distance. "Edison Palmer, you'll come with us please."

Mr. Palmer, more confused than ever, said, "I'm not going anywhere till I get some answers. What is going on here and what has happened to Alexis?"

"Ms. Coffey was severely beaten last night," replied the SP. "We're looking for answers, too. We think you might be able to give us a few. Now if you'll please come with us...."

Mr. Palmer got quickly to his feet. "Can I see her? How badly is she hurt?"

"You'll get your answers when we start getting some of our own. Come with us, please." The policeman took Mr. Palmer's elbow and shepherded him through the hostile crowd and down the hallway.

"Pig!" spat the woman. "I hope you get it twice as

bad as you gave to Alexis!"

"What is with these people?" muttered Mr. Palmer. "Why do they think I had anything to do with this?"

"Right now you appear to be the man with the information," responded the SP. "There're a few folks who'd like to hear what you have to say."

After a short walk to the command center, Mr. Palmer was escorted into a conference room. General McIntyre, Dennis Schweigert and the President were seated, waiting for his arrival. "Thank you, gentlemen," said the President, addressing the Security Policemen. "That'll be all for now." Then he turned to his disconcerted guest. "Ed, it's good to see you. I hope you've been well these past few months?" Mr. Palmer nodded and the President continued. "Our apologies for the rude awakening. Please, have a seat."

"Somebody want to fill me in here?" said Mr. Palmer.

"Of course," said the President. "Mac, do you want the honors?"

McIntyre, red-eyed from lack of sleep and visibly upset, exercised great control in his presentation. "Mr. Palmer:" he began, "Last evening Mr. Schweigert and myself were sitting in the canteen when a very badly beaten Alexis Coffey dragged herself to us. She was not able to tell us anything about what happened to her. Dr. Fletcher seems to think that you might know something about this situation. Perhaps you'd like to start with your whereabouts last evening?"

"*How* badly beaten?" answered Mr. Palmer. "Will

she be OK? Is anything broken?"

"The general asked you where you were last night," interrupted Dennis. "We'd like to hear about that first."

Mr. Palmer looked irritated. "I was in my quarters with Reggie Hall and Mrs. Gilbert. We were up pretty late playing cards. I went straight to bed when they left. Now, you tell me what I want to know."

The President nodded at Dennis who got up and spoke quietly to the SP's waiting just outside the door. He then turned to Mr. Palmer. "As General McIntyre said, she's been hurt quite badly. Internal injuries, facial cuts and contusions, possible concussion, maybe a few broken bones. She's going to live but she's got a pretty unpleasant recovery period to look forward to. It would appear that she was having an intimate meeting with someone that went quite wrong. Since you are the acknowledged expert on her whereabouts and activities, we thought you might be able to help us find out who it may have been."

"Intimate meeting? *Alexis?*" Mr. Palmer was incredulous. "Forgive me, but that's just a little absurd. She refuses intimacy with anyone and everyone. I don't know if you're aware of this but she still thinks her fans are going to be lined up in that tunnel to welcome her back when we get out of here. Frankly that's been worrying me for some time now." His voice showed a tenderness and concern that caught the three men by surprise. "I don't know if I could name a single person who might want to hurt her."

"*Think*," said Dennis. "Anyone at all. Has anybody said anything bad about her that you may have heard?"

"Mr. Schweigert," said Mr. Palmer politely, "can you recall anyone saying anything *nice* about Alexis since she's been here? She is quite spoiled and completely accustomed to having her own way. That gets on peoples' nerves. She is not exactly courteous in her dealings with others. Outside of myself and a few others, you're going to be hard-pressed to find anyone to say anything nice about her. But to beat her? I don't know of anyone...."

"Interesting point, Ed," conceded the President. "But we still need a place to start. How about anyone who has taken a particular interest in her? Her habit patterns, her actions, anything like that?"

Mr. Palmer began answering in the negative when he was interrupted by a soft knock at the door. Dennis spoke in hushed tones with the Security Policeman and then closed the door again. The men looked expectantly at him.

"His story checks out. He was with Mr. Hall and Mrs. Gilbert till a little after midnight."

Mr. Palmer looked irritated. Mac apologized. "You must understand, Mr. Palmer, that we have to check out everything—to protect you as well as Ms. Coffey."

Dennis pushed ahead. "So you can't think of anyone who has taken an unhealthy interest in her?"

"No, nobody, really." He hesitated, doubtful.

"What...?" asked the President. "It could be helpful."

"Well, this was months ago. Quite a few months ago, actually. It's hardly worth mentioning." The three men waited expectantly. Mr. Palmer began speaking, looking at the floor. "I—I'm sort of a spaz when it comes to celebrity." This was an uncomfortable confession on his part and it wasn't coming easily. "I've tried to meet some famous people and it seems I've always been let down. When I heard that Alexis was here, I got pretty excited. I didn't want to end up disappointed again so I decided to just admire her, you know, from afar. Let others do the close-in stuff, you know?" The President urged him to continue. "There's a small group of Alexis watchers. People who just can't get enough of her—even in this place. Way back, when I was first getting to know the group, Dr. Zorbas started asking a bunch of questions about her." Schweigert, General McIntyre and the President all exchanged looks. "Now that I think about it, it was kind of creepy. But then all of a sudden he stopped asking questions and sort of dropped out of the group. It's really been quite a long time. I just assumed he'd moved on." Mr. Palmer was thoughtful. "You know he did try to introduce himself—like he thought he might want to date her—when we first got here...."

"Tell us about that," prompted the general.

"Well, according to the people who were there and saw it happen, he tried to come on to her one evening at dinner. She shot him down pretty completely. It sounded absolutely humiliating, to tell you the truth. I think it was after that that he joined the Alexis watchers group. That's about it, really."

The President stood up. "Thank you, Ed. Once again, I apologize for dragging you out of bed for this experience. I hope you'll forgive us."

Mr. Palmer stood also and was joined by the others. "Do you think I can see her, sir?"

The President thought for a moment. "Well, she's in pretty bad shape but, if the doc says it's OK, I don't see why not."

"All things considered," added McIntyre, "she could probably do with someone to talk to. She's very much alone now. I have a feeling that some company might do her some good."

Mr. Palmer looked relieved. "I'll go now," he said.

As he was walking out the door the general took his arm lightly. "Son..." he said. "Doctor Fletcher thinks she may have been raped. Be very, very gentle with her."

Mr. Palmer's eyes widened in horror.

"Go on, son. She could use a friend. Just understand that it could take a while."

Karl Roscoe

E dison Palmer tiptoed quietly up to Alexis' bedside. Her breathing was labored and sounded as though she had something stuck in her windpipe. Her face was so swollen that he almost couldn't tell that it was her. Dr. Fletcher had cleaned her up a bit. The cleaning had exposed a large, ugly gash that started beneath her left eye, crossed the bridge of her nose and continued down just beneath the line of her right cheekbone. Apparently the doctor was trying to keep from having to stitch the skin back together and had applied a number of butterfly bandages. Unfortunately, it was readily apparent to even a non-medical observer that stitches would be required. That would change Alexis' face for the rest of her life.

She made a small noise and shifted slightly in the

bed. Mr. Palmer looked back at Dr. Fletcher for reassurance. She met his eyes with a small, encouraging smile. "She's in a lot of pain right now," said Carmen, "but I've sedated her to help her through the worst of it."

Mr. Palmer took a chair from by the door and dragged it to Alexis' bedside. There he sat, shocked, by what had happened to this young woman. "Thank you. Again, doctor."

Carmen nodded at him and gave the same slight smile. "God knows she could use somebody who cares about her," she thought. Though many had come by just to look, only one person that night had asked if she would be allowed to see anyone. "Jackals," she thought. "This guy actually looks as though he cares about her."

The Security Policeman had stopped by the infirmary to keep Carmen up to date on the inquiry so she wasn't surprised to see Mr. Palmer show up at the door. In fact, when he had come in, she saw that he was visibly shaken by the news. It seemed to her that his concern was different from everyone else's. He wasn't asking in a media-event sort of fascination. It was more like the way a father might ask about a child. Protective. Jealous. With a just a hint of anger in the background. This man, she thought to her small surprise, would do Alexis no harm. And he may possibly even do her a little bit of good.

Mr. Palmer sat forward on his chair, hunched over Alexis — but not too close. He ached to reach out — to touch her. The closest he could manage was to place his hand palm down on the sheet next to her arm. That would be enough for him right now.

Carmen watched him a moment more and then turned back to her quandary. This was extremely odd. She knew exactly how many syringes, bandages, tubes of anti-fungal cream and bottles of Amoxicillin were in the locked medical cabinet. But there were quite a few things missing. One small case was missing as well. No-one had broken in to the cabinet: There was no sign of forced entry at all. A creeping dread began to appear in the far recesses of her mind. To help her sort it out she began taking stock of everything. If there were medications being taken from the infirmary, perhaps the thief had taken other things as well.

After 15 minutes of searching she found only a few select medicines and bandages missing. They were the exact sorts of things one would need for an extended trip in the backwoods. The exact things that a doctor would have chosen to take. She called a volunteer over and asked him to have General McIntyre stop by. She sat in a nearby chair and fretted, watching Mr. Palmer watch Alexis. It did not take long for the general to arrive. And it seemed he'd been doing some investigating of his own.

"Doctor," he began. "You asked me to come by?"

"Yes, Mac. There are quite a few medical supplies missing from the case. Antibiotics, bandages...the kinds of things someone might want to take with them on a camping trip."

The general narrowed his eyes. "And you think that this might be a specific someone?" he ventured.

She took a deep breath and then looked squarely at him. "Yes. The missing items are exactly those that a doctor would choose to take." She watched closely for any signs of surprise but the general indicated none.

"Well," he said. "This is hardly even worth calling an investigation. Our good doctor has vanished and all the signs seem to be pointing right at him."

"All the signs?" repeated Carmen. "You've found more?"

"Based on what we already knew, I felt that we should have an immediate conversation with Doctor Zorbas. But it would appear that he doesn't want to be found. The SP's that I sent to locate him found only a few of his things left scattered around his quarters. Almost as though he grabbed only what he could carry and in a hurry. The cooks tell me that there were about a dozen MRE's left out on the counter this morning—and at least as many missing from the stocks. I've asked for a general search of the base but so far no-one has seen or heard from him since yesterday afternoon. Perhaps most disturbingly, someone has taken a bag full of cold weather survival gear from stores. I don't know how he thinks he's going to get past a 25-ton sealed steel door but it would appear that he's done a bit of planning already."

Carmen shook her head slowly and said, almost to

herself, "Mark...what have you done?"

Karl Roscoe

It was inevitable that Mark Zorbas would be caught. There was simply no long-term hiding in a four-acre complex with almost fifteen hundred people looking for him. After three days of eluding the searchers, he was finally trapped in a far recess of the reservoirs. The residents were less than kind when they dragged him back into the complex. Although he was athletically fit and capable of putting up significant resistance, he allowed them to kick and punch him on the short walk back to the survivors' community.

Having been notified of the arrest, the President was waiting in the Command Center. Watching their vicious treatment of Mark caused his anger to flare. He spoke sternly to his captors. "I will remind everyone here that this man is innocent of any crime until he is *proven* to be guilty."

The admonition was met with grumbling but they stopped the abuse. For his part, Mark remained stoic, impassive. He gave no outward indication of what he was thinking or how he was feeling.

"Doctor Zorbas, you are hereby formally charged with the beating of Alexis Coffey. Your trial will commence five days hence in the community center. Representation and consultation will be provided if you so wish. You will have that time to prepare your defense. In the meantime, you will be confined behind locked doors for your protection and the protection of the residents of this shelter."

The guards roughly led Mark through the hallways to a small room with nothing but a blanket and a small steel bucket inside. Once there, he sat quietly on the floor. From the moment of his discovery he hadn't said a word. Neither did he plan to speak until the trial. He had finally come up with a plan to escape from the mountain. These people would be his key to liberation.

"I still don't get it," Alexis was saying. "What exactly do you get out of this?" She lisped around her swollen tongue and whistled through her broken tooth when she spoke. It had been a week since the rape.

Edison Palmer smiled self-consciously. "Guess it just makes me feel good," he replied. Without looking at her he asked "So...do you still want me to leave?"

Alexis thought for a minute. She opened her mouth to say something and then closed it. She thought for another minute. "What are you planning for us to do?" She couldn't help but sound harsh when she asked. Almost as if she was accusing him of something.

"Nothing. Something. Anything. I don't know!" he laughed, ignoring her tone. "Pretty dorky, huh?"

"As a matter of fact, yes. It *is* dorky." She frowned but only slightly. Her swollen face was incapable of movement without a great deal of pain.

"Do you know how to play 'King the Corner?'" he advanced.

"Kind of risky, don't you think?" said Alexis. She wasn't yet finished with her interrogation. "Hanging around with me can be pretty emotionally damaging. I'm not exactly known," she said wryly 'for being an excellent companion."

"I'll take my chances," said Mr. Palmer. "So here's how we set it up. Ready?"

Carmen Fletcher was watching the exchange from across the room. The doctor in her was delighted to see the resilience with which her patient was starting her recovery. The psychiatrist in her was dismayed to see the compartmentalization of the pain going on behind the mask. She mentally crossed her fingers for both the patient and the benefactor. Each had a long road ahead.

Tomorrow morning was the trial. Alexis was aware of the fact but had said nothing. Physically she would be able to attend. Carmen was very concerned about her mental state. Would she be able to face the man who had attacked her—*allegedly* attacked her—so soon after the event?

Midway through his instructions for the card game, Alexis interrupted Mr. Palmer. "They're going to send him out there, aren't they?"

His easy smile hardened immediately. "I'm not sure

we should be talking about this."

Alexis persisted. "At the trial tomorrow. They're going to decide to get rid of him, aren't they?"

"All I can tell you," he answered, with a great deal of self control, "is that I don't think he deserves to stay. Not after what he did to you." He wasn't able to look at her as he said the words, though he knew she was watching him closely.

"What's with you?" she demanded. It was less than harsh—more like sincere curiosity. "Honest to God, you don't know anything about me. I could be an axe murderer or a junkie or an alcoholic or even a manic depressive. There's enough of those back home.... Why would you want to be my friend? Truly, what's in it for you?"

Still looking at the cards, he answered slowly and thoughtfully. "I can't give you an acceptable answer. I mean, you're beautiful. That goes without saying."

Her hand swept toward the gash in her face, fingertips brushing the new stitches in the scabby mess. "OK, *that's* bullshit! Can you not see what I look like?"

"No, I mean on the *inside*. And don't worry: You'll be beautiful on the outside again soon enough. The thing is, I've been looking for something magical in famous people. Something special that sets you apart from all of us. So far I've been pretty let down by what I've found. But I think you're different. At least I hope you are. And I want to get to know you to prove that I can be right about this."

She looked dubious. "You know I won't be able to hang around with you when we get back out there," she said with a nod in the direction of the door.

"I know," he said, looking at her now. "I know that." His eyes were sad as he faced her.

She zeroed in on that sadness. "What?" she said. "Do you think you *should* be able to hang with me and my friends?"

"No!" he replied quickly. "No, you should decide what you are going to do with your life once you get out."

Her eyes narrowed. "And you're about to tell me that there's no-one there waiting for us to come out, right? That I need to get over this idea of mine?"

"All I'm going to tell you is that you are ignoring that Jack right there and, if you don't do something about it, I will." He pointed at the card in question.

"You're evading," she observed.

"So?" he countered. "Right now I'm trying to do everything I can to keep you on an even keel. So what if people say there's no-one left out there? You've just been through a pretty ugly experience. Why don't we concentrate on getting you healed up before we take on the whole world."

She contemplated his face and his words silently. "Fine," she said. "Let's take care of that Jack, then."

T̲he Grabowski trial didn't even register on the social scale compared to the turnout for the trial for Dr. Mark Zorbas. It wasn't really possible to stuff more humanity into that room and the surrounding hallways, but it happened anyway. The compressed bodies created a sweaty heat in the room that only accentuated the stress in the air. The security escorts had a difficult time pressing through the throng with the prisoner. The animosity and malice from the crowd was palpable. Zorbas appeared completely emotionless.

"Order!" called the President. "Let the man through. This proceeding will be orderly." He looked sternly at the hostile crowd.

The people very reluctantly made a space for the three men. The escorts turned Zorbas to face the people in front of a solitary chair. Alexis was sitting off to his left, her face was stony and bitter. Mr. Palmer stood next to her, providing whatever moral support he could. Against the wall between the accuser and accused stood the President and General McIntyre.

It sounded like a beehive in that room. There was a harsh buzzing of voices filling the space with sound. The anger hanging in the air was fueled by the body heat. Everyone was sweating. In just a short time the smell of locker room permeated the air.

"Order!" repeated the President. "We will give the defendant a fair and unbiased trial. Preconceptions are not welcome here. When we have order we will get underway."

Slowly, very slowly, the noise died down.

"Thank you," said the President. "Let us begin." Turning to face him, the President said, "Mark Zorbas, you stand accused of assaulting and raping Ms. Alexis Coffey. Do you wish to enter a plea?"

Mark stood impassively and silently facing the survivors. He neither spoke nor moved.

"Very well," said the President. "We'll begin the trial. General McIntyre will present the people's case."

Mark sat down on the chair facing the crowd as McIntyre moved forward to present his findings. "On the night of June 17th, Alexis Coffey was attacked and molested by some person. Our investigation has indicated that the person most likely to have committed this crime is Doctor

Mark Zorbas. His motivation was simple: He wanted Ms. Coffey to be his companion. She refused; he beat her severely and then raped her. He then took a large ration of food, a portion of our drug supply and extreme weather gear; presumably to escape to the outside. I would like to begin by asking Ms. Coffey to present her story."

Almost unconsciously, Alexis reached out and grabbed Mr. Palmer's hand. She clutched it tightly, practically desperately. She locked eyes with McIntyre and began to speak. Without breaking eye contact with the general, nor physical contact with Mr. Palmer, she slowly, meticulously told what she remembered about that night. How he had locked them into that room together. How he had tried to seduce her with wine and food. How cruel his eyes became when she resisted. And then she couldn't remember. But she *hated* him. She told the people that she wanted him to die a horrible, painful death. When she was finished speaking, she broke eye contact with the general and stared straight ahead, setting her jaw hard. But she did not let go of Mr. Palmer's hand. She softened her grip. Just a little.

"A first person account," stated McIntyre, "of the events of that night. Doctor Fletcher:" he continued. "Can you tell us the result of your physical examination of Ms. Coffey on the night of the 17th?"

Carmen glanced at Alexis who bit her lip, then nodded slightly. "OK," said Carmen taking a deep breath. "When Ms. Coffey was admitted to my clinic I found defensive wounds characteristic of battering victims. There was also evidence of rape. Trauma, semen, some bleeding. Based on my professional opinion, I feel the evidence is incontrovertible. This woman was raped."

"Thank you, Doctor. Now, the final piece of evidence: Doctor Zorbas made himself scarce immediately after the incident. When he was finally found, in hiding, he had this bag," the general lifted the backpack before the crowd, "full of rations and survival gear. After a year of isolation in the safety and protection of this mountain, being well aware of the hostile conditions outside, what possible rationale could one individual have to need these items? I contend that the good Doctor had plans to escape to the outside and try to survive. He could thus avoid having to face responsibility for his actions and the judgment of his peers." He gazed across the faces gathered before him. Then, looking point blank at Mark, he said, "I rest my case."

The President turned to Zorbas. "Doctor Zorbas, do you wish to enter a plea at this time?"

Mark was a brick wall.

"You understand Doctor that, by refusing to enter a plea, the jury members have no other option than to assume your guilt...."

Again, no response.

"I see," said the President. "In that case, I should like to open this case for general discussion. You will," he reminded, "keep your remarks civil."

It became clear immediately that the verdict was unanimous. Mark Zorbas was guilty of raping Alexis Coffey. There was no need to belabor the discussion. The next order of business was to consider his punishment.

"Kill the son of a bitch," said a man in the front.

"Animal!" chimed in a woman. "Killing him's too good."

There was much of this talk. The general consensus was that Mark should receive the maximum punishment conceivable. Then a lone voice of dissent spoke out. "He is our only doctor," said Cookie Grabowski. "It may just be a matter of practicality, but who will care for us if we get ill and he's been cast out?"

The whole conversation took a sharp turn at this point with some taking the stand that regardless his position and knowledge, his actions warranted maximum punishment. Others questioned whether Doctor Fletcher wasn't fully suited to care for them, followed by a back and forth over Carmen's professional qualifications. Last, and by far the fewest, were the ones who hadn't considered this line of thought and were reconsidering the whole span of possible punishments.

There was a long and very contentious discussion but, in the end, the survivors decided to cast Mark out of the enclave. They elected to give him food enough for three days and one set of cold weather survival gear. There was a particularly bitter fight over these items. Alexis and the harshest of his critics wanted him to be banished naked into the cold. Leah Sandon managed to persuade the majority of the jurists that, although they could not abide by having him live among them any longer, they could simply not evict him without any chance of survival whatsoever. So it was by a clear majority of votes, Mark Zorbas was sentenced to be banished from the mountain. Those who were looking saw a small, smug smile briefly cross his lips. Mark felt he'd won.

The punishment was effective immediately. The crowd thronged around the court party as they escorted Mark to the door. Everyone wanted a glimpse of the outside. Alexis was near the head of the drove, waiting to see this awful man receive his punishment. She was satisfied at his sentence but, at the same time, dismayed. This day she would find out, once and for all, if there was anyone left alive outside. She was torn—she needed to see Mark ousted but petrified that she would be proven wrong. With leaden feet she marched with the rest to the door.

It took an interminably long period for the workers to get the door open. When it finally cracked around the seal there was a slight hiss of equalizing pressure. A bit of snow and frost blew in around the edges as the door swung inward. Impossibly cold air blasted the group standing by the door. The inrushing air smelled sulfurous—like tens of thousands of rotting eggs. The guards roughly shoved Mark out into the tunnel. They stood in the bitter chill looking up toward daylight. Others crowded around the doorway, fighting for a glimpse. Alexis couldn't help herself. She had to look. She stepped across the threshold and saw Mark Zorbas walking briskly into what appeared to be a refrigerator. There was a thick layer of frost encasing the tunnel. Drifts of snow had made their way even this deep down the entrance. As Mark disappeared into the gloom it became agonizingly clear that he was the only living thing on this part of the planet. The chill she felt from the outside air was nothing compared to the icy stab in her soul. She knew now that she was nothing. That there was no one left to worship her. Everything she had been vanished in that one instant.

Mr. Palmer gently pulled her back inside so they could close the door but she didn't feel his touch. She didn't feel anything anymore.

Karl Roscoe

Viktor Kasparof stood on a bluff overlooking the eastern edge of Colorado Spring's suburbs. It had taken forty-two days since their crash landing to struggle through the deep drifts of soot and ash and dirty gray snow. Many times they were forced by the cold to camp out in a house they'd found along the way for countless days. They were frozen, dirty and sick. But they had made it.

Viktor was studying the bloodied bandage covering his right wrist and hand. "Smells. Bad." He staggered in the drifts as he waved the appendage at Antonio DiGiammo. "I think is time to cut it off now."

DiGiammo gazed into the afternoon gloom and coughed. Clouds of steamy breath chased one another as cough followed cough in the ridiculously frigid air. They were both coated with a fine gray dust that had settled in every wrinkle, every pore—every part of their existence. "Perhaps now, Viktor," he said in a tired voice. "We've reached Colorado Springs. There will be hospitals here. We can use the equipment we find there." He looked at Kasparof's haggard face. "I'll cut it off for you," he said, nodding at the gangrenous appendage. "Now that we've made it. And then we'll find the others." He weakly patted his companion on the shoulder. "We'll tell them our story, no?"

Life continued in the mountain as it had before. The events set in motion by Mark Zorbas had created more than a few days' stir. It took a couple of weeks to settle back into the daily routine but eventually the same day-in, day-out returned. The survivors went back to hunkering down and waiting for the outside world to warm up enough to leave the base. Then they could deal with the impossibility of trying to restart human life on Earth.

Following her discovery that her life would never again be what it was, Alexis withdrew completely. She didn't speak. She refused interaction. Nothing, it seemed, would bring her out of her funk. As if to add to the black pit of despair that had become her life, Alexis discovered that she was pregnant with Mark Zorbas' baby; a discovery that only served to push her further away from the others. She disregarded the unborn child even more than she did herself, if that was possible.

Mr. Palmer's objective of becoming a friend to her had gone from being a long-shot to being flat out impossible. She shunned his attempts to interact with her. She closed her mind to the world around her. The self-imposed quarantine she had created during the first year of their confinement could only be seen as training for this new stage of isolation.

To say that Mr. Palmer suffered rebuke would be grossly overstating her actions. She merely ceased to acknowledge his or anyone else's existence. Despite her refusal to participate in any form of society, he ignored her withdrawal and maintained his involvement with their newfound friendship. In fact, had it not been for his efforts, neither Alexis nor the baby would have survived. Mr. Palmer brought her food, laundered her bedding and clothes and talked to her every day. The relationship became much like that of a grown child taking care of an Alzheimer's-stricken parent. Though the beneficiary couldn't completely appreciate what was being done for her, without that care the withered remains of her life would slowly crumble away. Mr. Palmer cheerfully fulfilled the role with support from virtually everyone in the mountain.

Volunteers came out of the woodwork. It seems that they were all just waiting for a tragedy to befall Alexis so they could offer their services as a sort of payback for her earlier mistreatment of them. Alexis was better fed, better cared for—nurtured, in fact—than she had ever been in her twenty-five years. Carmen was indispensable in providing pre-natal care. Under her steady guidance, the baby never had to want for any of its in-utero requirements.

Carmen had offered help in the early stages. Her first offer was to assist in the event that Alexis would want to end the pregnancy. Alexis was silent. She wouldn't acknowledge Carmen or her questions. She even refused eye contact. This frustrated the doctor greatly. She had lost one patient this year to self-imposed neglect. That would not happen again.

Without a yea or a nay, Carmen couldn't choose any drastic sort of intervention so she opted instead to do everything she could to ensure that this would be a healthy baby, born into a supporting community. Despite her efforts to ignore herself and her unborn child to death, Alexis was carried, day by day, into the future.

Leah Sandon recognized that the residents would need some sort of distraction to keep them from going stir-crazy. To occupy herself as much as for everyone else, she began to make a production of any and all holidays she could remember. In order to help them get past the recent trial and its aftermath, she chose July 4th as her first celebration. Not too many of the residents felt like celebrating but, in the end, were grateful for the diversion. Fireworks were obviously out of the question. However, with a heaping helping of enthusiasm, the survivors found ways to recreate the fourth. There were streamers, plastic bag balloons and extra rations of sweets. Spirits were greatly lifted. At the end of the celebration people were talking about which holiday they could celebrate next.

By October, Halloween was an occasion eagerly anticipated by all. In all, there weren't more than thirty children in the mountain but these thirty children had never had it so good. Fifteen hundred doting parents, all looking out for their future—for the future of their race through these small people. Halloween was a delightful excuse to spoil these kids completely. Everyone wanted to wear some kind of costume. Adult creativity was rampant. Here was an excuse to recover just a bit of the spirit of their former lives. They all chose stations from which they could open a door to hear the children shout "Trick or Treat!" Though there way no way the children could get to each of the doors in the one day allotted, the grownups remained hopeful that they would be chosen for the evening's honor. Bragging rights from a child's compliment on their costume were very highly regarded on the morning after.

Thanksgiving came around and all the survivors pooled the special treats they'd been saving for themselves. The community was pulling more tightly together with each holiday orchestrated by Leah. Her position as their spiritual shepherd was now cemented and her confidence grew daily. It was a remarkable responsibility to be the vessel into which these people poured their faith. She flourished as they continued to spill the strength of their belief into her.

March was difficult—St. Patrick's day was a challenge for a liquorless group trapped underground. Fortunately it was the day Alexis' baby had chosen to be born. The residents were elated at the news of the infant's arrival. More importantly, Alexis herself appeared to wake up. The delivery went remarkably smoothly. Carmen had expected a number of complications and difficulties, if for no other reason than that it was Alexis giving birth, but they never appeared. After a mere five hours of labor, Alexis pushed a new human being out into the mountain refuge. Carmen placed the baby immediately onto Alexis' bare breast to suckle. For the first time in almost a year Alexis finally showed some emotion. And that emotion was a smile. The baby, paradoxically, had given life to Alexis.

She had a daughter; a baby girl. The child brought a spark of delight to the whole mountain base. Everyone came by to look at her and dote on her. In a complete turnaround, Alexis not only accepted the visitors but actually welcomed them. It was a shock to everyone...even to Alexis herself. Incredibly, during her long silence she had been healing herself—healing her own mind. The first time she laid eyes upon the child she felt an up surging of optimism.

It also appeared that Alexis had decided to accept Mr. Palmer as the baby's de-facto father and her partner. She understood subconsciously that he had been there for her every single day. She decided consciously that she wouldn't mind having someone like that around for each of the days to come. The residents were stunned at the change in Alexis and delighted to welcome her into their community. After the horrible events which had led to their entrapment, the survivors began to feel that might be a real possibility of seeing the light of a new day for humanity. The sun, which was trying to break through the choking clouds of dust outside, had begun, figuratively, to penetrate the inside of their haven.

Alexis and Mr. Palmer decided to name the girl Nadja, in honor of her mother's grandmother. It is a Russian word, meaning hope—a decision happily received by the residents of Cheyenne. Spring was bringing the promise of new life—of a new chance.

B ill Grabowski had had a headache for three days now and the diarrhea was getting worse. Cookie finally harangued him to the point where he decided go to the clinic. "Doc Fletcher around?" he asked the attendant on duty.

"Sure," said the man. "She's in the back with a patient right now." He slid a clipboard with several pieces of colored paper over to him. "If you would, just fill out these forms and give me a copy of your insurance card...."

"Wise guy," growled Grabowski. "I'm not really in the mood, thanks."

The man grinned and said, "Just trying to keep it light! Seriously though, the doc would like you to write your symptoms on one of those sheets. Any color will do but I've been asking folks to try to match the paper color to how they feel."

"Keep your day job," said Grabowski, pulling the clipboard out of the man's grasp.

"I'll tell Doctor Fletcher you're here," said the man cheerfully.

A few moments later Carmen walked out of the examining room followed by Dennis Schweigert. "Mr. Grabowski...good afternoon. I'll be right with you." Then to Dennis she said: "Three times a day for two weeks. I'll help you remember." She kissed him lightly on the cheek. "See you tonight."

As an unhappy looking Dennis brushed past Grabowski she turned to him and said, "How may I help you today?"

He handed Carmen the clipboard and said, "I'm pretty miserable right now, doc."

"So Steve tells me," she said with a grin and a nod toward the attendant. Glancing down the sheet of paper her smile waned. "Hmmm. You seem to have the same bug as Dennis. Come on back. We'll take a look at you."

After a brief exam she prescribed the same treatment she had for Schweigert and sent Grabowski on his way. On his way out Grabowski almost bumped into Colonel Jack Wilkes. He met the other man's hard look of disgust and pushed past him to the corridor. Wilkes said in a voice loud enough to be overheard, "You're not actually helping to keep that worthless piece of crap alive, are you doc?"

"My job is to keep all of us alive and healthy, Mr. Wilkes. Is there something I can help you with?" she answered testily. She didn't have much patience for petty disputes—regardless the emotional content.

After taking care of Wilkes' request she continued with her business. Seeing two identical cases so close together caused her to check her stored cache of medicine. She reassured herself that she had an adequate supply for any small calamity that they may encounter and went on with her day.

The following morning she saw five more patients with similar complaints. A dozen more came trickling in throughout the afternoon and early evening. For the next three days she was inundated with patients, all exhibiting the same symptoms, all receiving the same prescription. On the morning of the sixth day she found herself waking with the same well-described headache and diarrhea. Fortunately the epidemic appeared to have run its course by that time. Since there were only one or two new cases to evaluate, she opted to stay in bed that day and let her assistants care for the stragglers.

She woke that next morning and almost didn't wait to get cleaned up before she checked her drug stocks again. It was as bad as she feared: The run on the clinic had seriously depleted her reserves. With what she had remaining she estimated she had only enough for an additional 20 or so cases. Carmen went in search of McIntyre and the President immediately. She found them sitting at a table conversing easily in the galley.

At her approach the President said pleasantly, "Here comes our doctor now. Looks like you've had your hands full for the last week or so!"

Carmen offered a small, curt smile in return. "Gentlemen," she said tightly. "I'm afraid I have some bad news." McIntyre raised an eyebrow and the two men waited expectantly for her to continue. She didn't delay. "We have a serious shortage in our supply of medications. I'm not comfortable with what we have left on hand."

"Well," mused the President, "we only have two or three months left before we get out of here...what's the likelihood we'll need more in that time?" He looked to McIntyre for support. "I mean, we've been down here for almost two years and this is the first real opportunity we've had to use them."

"Good health is not the kind of thing I like to gamble with," responded Carmen tersely.

"Understood," replied McIntyre. "So what do you have in mind, doc?"

"Carmen looked at him blankly. "What do you mean, 'what do I have in mind?' I'm just telling you that we have a serious problem here."

"OK," agreed the general. "We understand that you have a problem. Now, that puts us in something of a unique position here. Your problem is a shortage of medicines. We have no replacements in this facility. My understanding is that you want to get more to replenish those we've had to use. This presents a quandary. How is it that you propose we solve it?" He was sitting placidly in his chair with his hands folded comfortably across his belly but she could see that his mind was working swiftly behind his gray eyes.

She was flummoxed. She was the doctor, not the problem solver! "I.... Well.... I.... Hell, I don't know!"

"We sympathize with your problem Carmen but there doesn't seem to be any rational solution presenting itself," said the President.

She decided to dig in. "You do understand that this is *our* problem. Everyone's; not just mine."

McIntyre fielded this one. "And you understand that, regardless who owns the problem, the solutions are all unfeasible?"

"What about sending someone out to look for more?" she said. "I don't expect that it could be that difficult. There are, what, six hospitals in Colorado Springs?"

The President shook his head. "It's April, Carmen. You know as well as the rest of us — better even — that it's an icebox out there. Just ask Dennis."

"He's right, doc," chimed in McIntyre. "You know we can't leave here until high summer at the earliest. Who is it that you plan to ask to risk their life just to give you a little piece of mind?"

"I don't think you gentlemen appreciate the gravity

of the situation," she reiterated.

McIntyre responded. "I disagree. I think we have a complete grasp of the dilemma. But I'm afraid I'm with the President on this one. Luck should be on our side for the next couple of months.

She looked skeptical.

"Really Carmen," the President said soothingly. "It's far too dangerous." He leaned back in his seat. The decision had been made. "I'm quite certain that we'll make it through the next few months with no more incidents." McIntyre nodded in concurrence. "And, in truth, you *do* have a small supply left. It's not like you have nothing at all...."

With a frustrated sigh she threw up her hands and stomped back to the clinic.

"What do you think, boss? Is this something we're going to regret?" asked McIntyre.

"I hope not, Mac," said the President sincerely. "Just a few more months and we're home free."

Two weeks passed and so had the bug. Almost all of the stricken survivors had completely recovered. Pretty much everyone forgot the incident. It was in that forgetful lull that the disease came roaring back. Late one afternoon five new cases appeared. Seven more came to the clinic through the night. Carmen prescribed the last of her precious medication by noon of the next day. She was furious. She came looking for the President to give him a piece of her mind. Her satisfaction was nipped in the bud when she found him in as bad or worse condition than the others. He got to be the first one to find out that there were no more drugs to ease his suffering. Wincing through his pain, the President attempted to joke about his predicament but Carmen's face was a testament to the seriousness of the situation.

She did what she could to ease his suffering but, without the medicine, she was limited to head-patting and platitudes.

Leaving him, she proceeded directly to General McIntyre's quarters. She still needed to vent. She stormed into his room, preparing to let him have both barrels. Apparently he'd been told she was enroute. He was already way ahead of her.

"Save your breath, doc," he said, with his palms facing her. "We screwed up. You were right."

"I don't want to be right, Mac," she fumed. "I want these people to be healed." She stood in front of him with her hands on her hips. "I suppose you already know that the President is sick?"

"I did not know that," he answered, alarmed. "You've started his treatment I assume...."

"Nope," she said matter-of-factly. "I'm flat out. I've got nothing left to give."

McIntyre was instantly agitated. "He's the President," he said. There was no equivocation. "He's a priority!"

"Priority or no, I'm *out*, Mac. I don't *have* anything to give him," she repeated.

"Then you get them from someone else," insisted McIntyre. He was growing angry that she wasn't comprehending the order. This was a simple problem with a simple solution.

"You can't be serious," said Carmen, incredulous.

"I *am* serious. He's the President. He's our priority.

He'll get the medication." McIntyre was firm.

Carmen folded her arms across her chest. "My clinic," she said testily "is based on need, *not* priority. If you want him to receive treatment, you can just go find some volunteer to give up their own medication. Good luck finding someone to opt to be sick just so the President can be healthy." She was as resolute as McIntyre was firm. "Don't expect me to get involved in that kind of insanity." She spun on her heel and marched back to the clinic, more dissatisfied with her mission now than when she set out.

McIntyre wasted no time in getting to the President's side. Due to the symptoms, this turned out to be a fairly regrettable choice. The man in question was in the throes of involuntary evacuation of the contents of his bowels. He wasn't enthralled with the thought of entertaining at that particular moment. Beating a hasty retreat, McIntyre struck out to find a substitute who would be willing to sacrifice their own health for that of the President. He went to bed late that night after a fruitless search. After only a few hours of sleep he awoke with a pounding headache and a disconcerting gurgle in his gut.

Just four days into the epidemic a little over half of the population was incapacitated. The entire Grabowski family was out of commission. Bill had already run his course of therapy weeks earlier. Apparently he'd built up an immunity to the disease. He did his best to ease his family's suffering. For the most part though, all he could do was watch.

Colonel Wilkes, along with about a hundred others, appeared to be naturally immune. He made himself busy as a runner for the clinic. Another couple hundred or so got a mild case; over after just a few short, but troubled hours. In all, almost eight hundred people were becoming seriously ill in a fragile, closed environment. Carmen was the only one who could foresee just how critical the situation was becoming.

On the fifth day, someone actually died. She was an older woman, in her late sixties. Carmen didn't yet consider it to be a harbinger exactly, but she was deeply concerned and began to pay closer attention. By day six two more survivors had perished. Drastic measures now had to be considered. She sought out Colonel Wilkes with the proposal she had offered to the President and McIntyre two weeks earlier.

"So that's pretty much our only chance to fix this?" he asked.

"Unless you know how to manufacture the stuff," she answered honestly. "I don't like this any better than you do, Jack but, if we don't do something soon, an awful lot of people are going to start dying."

He thought for a moment. "Orlando. Major Gomez: Is he sick too?"

"Can't tell you off the top of my head," said Carmen. She was tired, distracted and didn't feel much like focusing on others' problems at that moment.

"I can trust him," said Wilkes. "If I'm going to be risking my kiester, I'd just as soon have him along watching out for me."

"Sorry I can't help," Carmen shrugged. It seemed that she had been pushed beyond the ability to care. "Maybe I can ask around...." She was every bit as exhausted with this epidemic as she had been back in Cody when this had all begun.

"I'll go find out myself," said Wilkes brusquely. "Get a list of what you want and where to find it. I'll make it happen."

Wilkes found Major Gomez. Armed with Carmen's wish-list they struck out for Colorado Springs' hospitals and pharmacies. Few of the survivors were aware of the bold attempt being initiated by these two men. They were less than three hours out the door when General McIntyre died.

Karl Roscoe

Bill Grabowski sat wretchedly contemplating his wife's face. She was staring blankly at the ceiling in their quarters. She would not acknowledge his presence. She had been dead for eighteen hours.

Her death had been preceded by that of his son and had followed that of his daughter and her husband. In the past 24 hours he had lost everything in this life that ever mattered to him. Now, shell-shocked, he stared into Cookie's face. Not knowing what else to do, he cursed the doctor and the drugs that had saved his life. Cursed the fact that he'd been allowed to live. What value was there in continued existence without Cookie? This was the question he was asking himself and the empty eyes of the dead woman before him.

"Mr. Grabowski?" said a quiet voice. "Mr.

Grabowski? I'm sorry.... I'm sorry about...." The man's voice trailed off. Bill sat, facing Cookie, doing his utmost to ignore the man in his quarters.

"Mr. Grabowski, it's the President. He's dying." The man was desperate. He had never embarked on an errand of this magnitude. He understood what was expected of him but was completely unsure how to follow it through successfully.

"He's insisting that he talk to you." Desperation was now seeping out of the man and into his voice. "Mr. Grabowski, I know this is difficult but can you come with me please? Please? It's very important."

With an immense effort Grabowski pulled his eyes away from Cookie's face. The man who had come for him was pale and very thin. He had obviously been through an attack of the disease. "What does he want with me?" rasped Grabowski. "What can I do?"

"He's pretty insistent," said the man. "There's nothing you can do..." he said, looking at the corpses laying about the room. "Here, I mean." The man faltered and looked miserable. The epidemic had destroyed the social fabric of the community. The simple dignity of being left alone to grieve for your dead was just another casualty of the disease. Nonetheless the man was conscious of the intrusive nature of his presence and request. He was keenly aware of the impact that his mere existence was having on this grieving husband. "Please..." said the man.

Grabowski sighed deeply. "Fine," he said without emotion. "Let's go talk to the President." The two men walked from Grabowski's quarters to the Command Center and the President. Along the way they passed bodies left lying in pools of their own filth. Neither paused to reflect about the souls lost—there were just too many gone. The entire complex was littered with the garbage of everyday life. No one was left to pick it up—daily survival was the only priority.

The man led him to a room near the back of the Command Center. Grabowski was appalled by the President's appearance. He looked like a holocaust survivor; gaunt, emaciated. He had become a mere wisp of the healthy subject he'd been only two weeks earlier. As Grabowski knelt by his side, the President had only the strength to acknowledge him with a nod. "Mr. President," he said. "You asked to see me?"

In a voice barely above a whisper the President spoke. "Bill," he said. "I'm done here." He closed his eyes and then opened them. "Mac's gone." He stopped, exhausted already from the effort. Gathering his strength to finish, he began again. "They need a leader, Bill. You have to do it."

Grabowski shook his head. "I'm not your guy," he said. "I've lost Cookie. Both kids. I don't even want to live myself, let alone lead these people. Sorry boss, but you'll have to find someone else."

The President looked intensely into his face. "*You*, Bill," he hissed. "You must lead them!" The words rang hard in the small room.

Grabowski continued shaking his head. "I can't," he repeated.

Harnessing the full power of his will, the President rolled himself onto his elbow and clutched at Grabowski's shirt. "Goddammit, Bill," he demanded. "We're dying. All of us! Get over it and *lead* them!" He collapsed in a wheezing mass, his energy spent. The little man who'd brought Grabowski stood silently, passively watching; waiting. He felt oddly detached but nonetheless curious about the outcome of this exchange.

Finally, Grabowski spoke. "OK," he said flatly. "I'll do it. But I'm going to do it *my* way."

Closing his eyes, the President mouthed the words "Thank you." Opening his eyes and gazing vacantly at the ceiling, he mouthed them silently again. "Thank you."

Finally, impossibly, Jack Wilkes and his friend Orlando Gomez came back to the mountain. They had been gone for six days. In that time over four hundred of the survivors had died; including the President, the Grabowski family and General McIntyre. The first thing they noticed on their way back into the complex was the stacks of bodies left in the tunnel. Hundreds of fellow survivors left neatly piled, lining the walls. These were the faces of the people they had come to know over the last year of confinement. It was a difficult homecoming to say the least.

It wouldn't get easier for Wilkes. He wasn't ten steps back inside when he found out that William Grabowski had been chosen by the President to be the successor. "Ho-ly Fuck!" he told the man assigned to sit by the door awaiting their return. "You have *got* to be shitting me."

"I'm not," replied the man. "He's been driving us all like dogs. 'Clean up your quarters!' 'Wipe down all the floors!' 'Take your corpses out into the tunnel!' God, what an asshole!"

"You don't need to tell me about it," growled Wilkes. "Where is he?"

"Don't know," said the man. "Seems like he's everywhere at once. Been kind of wild and scary since his family died. But the President wouldn't let anyone else lead. Whole thing's weird if you ask me."

Without further comment Wilkes and Gomez made straight for the infirmary. Carmen looked up from another hopeless case, saw them both and burst into tears. "Oh my God!" she cried. "Oh my God! You're back! You've made it!"

Gomez held his backpack up high. "We found it all. Everything you asked for. Syringes are on top. I assume you'll be wanting those first?"

"Yes!" she shouted, running across the small clinic to grab the bag. "I'll start right now!" She tore open the bag and began filling a syringe immediately.

"So, you made it," said Bill Grabowski, coming around the corner. "Good. We could use the help. Check the roster in the galley. You'll find your assignments there."

"Great to see you, too," said Wilkes. "We're just fine. Thanks for asking."

"We've all got a job to do here, Jack," snapped Grabowski. "This place is a stinking shithole of death. It's not about to fix itself. Rather than taking your personal vendetta out on me, I suggest you get to work." The two men glared angrily at one another. Turning to Carmen, Grabowski said, "Doctor, I don't guess I need to tell you what to do...." With one last sweep of his eyes across the clinic, he spun on his heel and charged down the hallway barking orders at whoever was unfortunate enough to cross his path.

Carmen left, racing down the hallway. A moment later Dennis Schweigert came in looking expectantly at the newcomers. "I heard you were back," he said. "Damn, I'm glad you guys made it!"

"So the President died and left him God?" asked Gomez derisively, with a wag of his head toward the door.

"Who, Grabowski?" said Dennis. "Yeah, he's got a bug up his ass." He changed the subject. "Forget him: Tell me about the outside—what's going on out there?"

"It's Hell," said Wilkes immediately. "You were right, Dennis. It is unbelievable out there."

"First night out I was sure we were going to die," said Gomez, shaking his head. "I never knew it was possible to be so cold on this planet."

"Raw, bitter wind, deep snowdrifts, constant twilight during the day. Never got above -30 degrees on any of the thermometers we could find. And at night it got *really* cold. No way we can survive out there right now," said Wilkes.

"What about life?" asked Dennis. "Any signs of life?"

Wilkes and Gomez exchanged a glance. "No," said Gomez. "Nothing out there."

"What...?" questioned Dennis. "What did you guys see?"

"Nothing for certain," said Wilkes. "Look, it's probably nothing at all."

"Well, what was it?"

"Somebody was alive out there," said Gomez. "It's hard to say how long ago it was, but we found some things that were a little spooky. Somebody survived out there for at least a little while."

"Damn," said Dennis.

"Now you tell us." interrupted Wilkes. "What's going on with that son of a bitch Grabowski? Where's Mac? What happened to the President?" The interrogation was coming fast and furious. "He's not really running this place, is he?" he asked incredulously.

"Mac died," replied Dennis. "He was one of the first to go. Surprised the hell out of all of us." The pain was evident on his face. Dennis had liked and respected the general. "Seems he had some heart problems he'd been keeping to himself, and the strain of the disease was too much for him."

Dennis was quiet for a moment, reflecting. Then he said, "The President hung in there for a long time. I actually thought he would make it, but I guess it was more than he could handle. He died day before yesterday." Dennis was a little wistful. Then he snapped out of his reverie and said, "And yes, he called Grabowski right after you two left to put him in charge. Bill didn't want the job. Told the President flat-out that he'd rather be dead." Now Dennis was matter-of-fact. "His whole family died the day before, you know." Again Wilkes and Gomez looked at one another. "Grabowski took it unbelievably hard. The guy who saw the President hand over power said the he was adamant that Grabowski be the one. I don't get it." Dennis stood with a hand on his hip, shaking his head and gazing at the ground. "Now it seems like Bill's pissed off at the whole world and he's taking it out on us."

"Speaking of which," continued Dennis, "I'm on the list for cadaver patrol. We're putting them outside for now. Guess you saw them all on your way in...."

"We did," nodded both men.

"So I've got to get back to it," said Dennis. "I figured that the clinic is always the best place to start looking. You guys are more than welcome to help, if you'd like...."

"Thanks, but I think we'd better try tracking down the chief," said Wilkes. "I expect he'll want to hear about what we found out there."

"Good luck," countered Dennis. "Handing out work orders is about as much as he ever says to anyone. Just don't expect any cozy little chats."

The two men took their leave and went in search of

Grabowski. He wasn't that difficult to find. They just had to follow the trail of angry, broken people he left crying or cursing in his wake.

"You want to know what we found out there, or what?" called Wilkes from behind.

Grabowski halted his stalking momentarily and turned. "Something I need to know about, or are you just looking to cry some more?"

"Fuck you," said Gomez.

"That's what I thought," answered Grabowski and started off down the hall again.

"There's somebody out there," said Wilkes. "Don't know if they're still alive, but someone was out there not long before we were."

Grabowski stopped and, only half turning around, said, "Not a surprise. We'll have to look into it. Meanwhile, you two get to the galley and find your work assignment." Then he was gone down the hall again.

"Asshole!" exclaimed Gomez.

"Hmmm," said Wilkes. He wasn't finished with the conversation yet.

B ill Grabowski was angry. The love of his life, the only person he'd ever cared about, was dead. He wanted to be with her. His choice was death with his wife over life with these irritating people. Instead he'd been given a direct order from the Commander in Chief. Though the President had removed him from the Army and stripped him of his rank, Grabowski had never ever stopped being an officer. Not in his heart. So when the President gave him the order to lead them, it superseded everything else in his life. And they both knew that it would.

The order was simple: Lead them. That meant one thing and one thing alone: Make absolutely certain that they survived. Make absolutely certain that there would be a humanity to carry on when the disease had passed. Grabowski understood what this meant and hated it. He hated the President for having done this to him. He hated the survivors for being there to prevent him from being with his beloved family again. But he had sworn an oath to follow orders and that was exactly what he would do. If it took his last dying breath, he would make it his only goal. His solitary purpose for existing would be that these people would once again see the light of day. It would not be pleasant for any of them.

First things were first. There were corpses everywhere. The complex was full of them. The stench of their rotting was beginning to saturate the air. They had to be removed. So that was step one: Put the dead in that giant refrigerator outside. They could be dealt with later—after survival was guaranteed. Next: The place was a hideous mess. Diarrhea and vomit were splashed everywhere. The residents had been too ill or too preoccupied with nursing duties to clean it all up. This place would be scrubbed thoroughly. Finally, they would need a new plan for evacuation of the base and population of the town. These people were about to become very, very busy.

He had given up eating. He slept only three hours each night since he'd received his new assignment. There was no time to lose. If the corpses were left on the inside, new disease would spread like wildfire. If the place wasn't cleaned up, the epidemic would continue indefinitely. So he had been prowling the hallways for the past six days searching for slackers, ordering those who were even moderately healthy to work, work and then work some more. There was no time to lose.

That Wilkes and Gomez had returned was good news. The medications they brought would stop the epidemic. Wilkes himself, he thought, would likely be a problem. The attempted coup, Wilkes' part in stopping it, the trial—all of this placed him firmly in opposition to Grabowski's leadership. He knew he'd have to deal with it at some point. Hopefully sooner rather than later. These kinds of things were best dealt with swiftly and surely.

As if on cue, Jack Wilkes and Orlando Gomez appeared around the next corner. They made a beeline straight for Grabowski.

"Looks like you got your wish after all," said Wilkes. "How's it feel to be in charge?"

"I'm not interested in discussing that," replied Grabowski curtly. He saw a woman cowering in a doorway. In her direction he said, "I saw about six more bodies in building three. Get over there and get rid of them."

"B-but I'm *sick*," she said, and she looked it.

"Get your ass over there, now," Grabowski intoned menacingly. "I don't want to see you here on my next sweep through." The three men marched ahead and she scampered off in their wake.

"So that's how it's going to be, then..." drawled Wilkes.

Grabowski stopped abruptly and spun to face him. "I'll tell you *exactly* how it's going to be, Jack." He put his face just inches away from Wilkes'. "I was placed in this position against my will. Quite frankly, I don't want the job. But I promised the President of the United States that I would do it. I'm under very specific orders to get these people out of here alive. I'm going to do that. You're going to help. Everyone will cooperate." The men were so close they could smell each other's breath. Neither backed away, even a fraction. "When that's all done and sorted out, you can come and get me. You can have an impeachment or arrest me or whatever the hell you want. For now, you, Gomez and everyone else is going to do exactly as I say. No delays, no bullshit. You got that?"

Gomez's face was a mask of shock. He hadn't quite expected such a vicious attack. Wilkes, on the other hand, drew himself up to his full height and stared right back at Grabowski. "OK, Bill," he said. "I'll do just that. And when we get out of here I'll be certain to insure you get your day in court. Again."

"Good," said Grabowski sharply. Then he charged off the hallway at a full clip. "Get over to the galley like I told you to, and check out the duty roster," he called over his shoulder. "We've got a lot of work to do and not much time to finish.

Carmen wasted no time in getting the drugs to the people. The worst cases got an immediate injection of antibiotics. As she was running from patient to patient she tossed bottles of oral meds to those who were less severe. It was unbelievably liberating for her to be able to *do* something. Standing-by, holding their hands and helplessly watching people die was beyond unacceptable.

Despite her best efforts, Cheyenne survivors continued to die. Some were too far gone and the drugs too late. Some had progressed into other diseases, triggered by the epidemic. A single doctor—psychiatrist turned MD no less—was simply no match for almost eight hundred sick people. She refused sleep; she rested only when Dennis hunted her down and forced her to take a break. Three days after the return of the explorers people were still dying by the tens. By this time over seven hundred of the residents had perished.

Bill Grabowski continued to stride through the hallways, finding more bodies; bullying the survivors into ridding the compound of those who hadn't lived. Without exception, everyone hated him. Fiercely. He neither acknowledged their plight nor cared. There was work to be done. If they were to survive, then it would be his responsibility to make it happen.

He had allowed a single concession in the work schedules: They could now elect to work together in teams of two or three. Jack Wilkes and his friend Orlando Gomez were hauling cadavers out together and talking.

"That guy's a pile of crap!" said Gomez through gritted teeth.

"He is, no doubt," puffed Wilkes. "But there may be something more to it. He may actually be doing us a favor."

"You gotta be shitting me," said Gomez. "Did you see what he did to that family last night? Freakin' Grandma had to carry her daughter's body out by herself. With Grabowski barking at her heels the whole way!"

"Hold on a sec," said Wilkes. "Let's put this down here." They lowered the body they were carrying to the floor. They both bent over to catch their breath, hands on their knees and panting slightly. After a moment Wilkes spoke again. "I don't like him, that's for sure. But have you been watching him?" Gomez shook his head. "It's like he's possessed." Wilkes was thoughtful for a moment. "I don't know. The way he's driving us, the way he's driving himself.... There's no question that he's not enjoying the slightest thing about being in charge."

"Nothing to enjoy, Jack," Gomez frowned. "Do you think you'd enjoy being the boss when all you can do is tell people to carry hundreds of dead bodies out into the snow?"

"No, that's not it." He stopped speaking when he heard voices. They both looked up as Mr. Palmer and Alexis Coffey approached, dragging a body behind them.

"Better not let the General catch you guys loafing," said Alexis, with her baby dangling in front of her. She was still feeling the effects of her recent bout with the disease, but was improving by the day.

"We just saw him back there," said Mr. Palmer dipping his head back toward the hall they'd just emerged from.

"I'm not too worried about that," said Gomez. "I'll just tell him where to go."

"How are you feeling, Alexis?" interrupted Wilkes. She didn't look great.

"I'll be OK," she answered. "About a thousand times better than I did. Thanks to you two...."

"How about the baby?" asked Gomez.

"She's good. It's kind of weird—Both Ed and I got hit hard, but Nadja never changed a whit. I think she's here to stay."

The two men grunted in satisfaction. It seemed that

after the epidemic no one smiled anymore. "You ready, Orlando?" asked Wilkes preparing to lift his end again.

"Gimme one minute," said Gomez, raising a forefinger.

"Sorry boys, but we're out of here," said Mr. Palmer. "We're going to try for five bodies today." He shook his head. "God, that sounds gross."

"It is what it is, babe," said Alexis. "Let's get going." They dragged their corpse ahead down the hallway.

"So you were saying?" said Gomez when the couple was out of earshot.

"Grab his ankles," said Wilkes. They hoisted the cadaver and he continued with his thought. "He's different." Breathing heavily from the effort, he theorized, "Maybe it was losing his family. Maybe it's being surrounded by all this death. Maybe he found Jesus or something. But the guy has changed."

"I doubt that seriously, Jack."

"Watch him, Orlando," continued Wilkes. "It's like somebody took all the life out of him and the only thing left now is getting us all out of here. You'll see what I'm talking about."

"I'm going to need to see it, Jack. I don't trust that guy. Not as far as I can throw *this*," he said, indicating the body between them.

For three weeks Grabowski had worked them like slaves. Nearly eight hundred people had died in that horrible epidemic and every single one of the bodies needed to be removed. Those who weren't on cadaver disposal duty were assigned to clean up. This wasn't light housekeeping — they spent entire days deep cleaning individual rooms within the buildings. It went on and on and on. Room after filthy room, building after building. Grabowski authorized the use of the rationed water for the cleaning operation. No one said so out loud but, with so many dead, rationing wasn't nearly as important as it had been. It became a simple fact of their new lives that supplies were no longer as tight as they had been before the epidemic.

Grabowski was merciless. ' He continued on his

rounds through the hallways, barking at everyone. In part because of his demeanor and in part because they could never really bounce back from the trauma, the residents' outlook changed dramatically. Where there once had been lightheartedness and occasional levity, there was now only a grim, businesslike approach to daily survival. Even the children, who had not long ago provided a welcome distraction from the reality of the survivors' situation, had an echo of the adults' dreadfully somber visage in their own faces. All life within the mountain had taken on a pragmatic, obligatory drone. They now practiced the vocation of survival for the sake of survival. Joy had vanished from their lives.

As he had promised Gomez, Jack Wilkes was keeping a close eye on Grabowski. While he didn't necessarily appreciate the tactics Grabowski was using, he admired the result. Their new leader had turned a hopeless situation into an opportunity. His brutality had forced the survivors into facing the reality of their situation and what they might expect in their new roles once outside the mountain. Quite simply, they all owed their very lives to William Grabowski — like it or not. Without explicitly stating the fact, Wilkes had become Grabowski's supporter.

Outside, the world was finally coming around. By late June the temperature had climbed into the forties during the day. The sky was beginning to clear and, at times, blue could be seen through the patches of dusty gray. Very little in the way of visible life was making any kind of comeback.

The rain that fell from the sky was still tainted with the sulfurous fallout. The acidic showers poisoned the soil just as Dennis had predicted. The earth was not making it easy for life to regain a toehold.

Despite strong protests from Orlando Gomez, Jack Wilkes began spending more time with Grabowski. He saw occasional glimpses of the man behind the mask. When a day had been particularly stressful or tiring, Wilkes could see the despair in Grabowski's face. On one occasion he'd overheard the leader whispering, "I'm coming, Cookie. Not long, now."

The more time he spent with the man, the more Wilkes began to understand the burden that Grabowski had undertaken. Surprising even himself, Colonel Wilkes began to take on some of Grabowski's duties. If Grabowski had noticed the help, he'd never acknowledged it. But he did begin to offer larger and larger chunks of responsibility to Wilkes. Eventually Wilkes became second-in-command of the mountain survivors. His approach toward the residents was different; softer. He applied a bit more mercy, thus becoming the good cop to Grabowski's bad. Together they shepherded the traumatized residents through the last few months underground. Soon it would be time for the ragged remains of this human tribe to return to the surface.

Karl Roscoe

The mountain's occupants were, at last, preparing to leave their home of the last two and a quarter years. Grabowski made certain they followed the plan put together by McIntyre and the President to the letter. This was the one testament to their former leaders that they could offer — to carry on by using the plan that they had envisioned. In one rare moment of conversation that included none of his characteristic snarling, Grabowski quizzed Dennis one more time.

"I know you've had this conversation with Mac and the President about a thousand times Dennis, but I need you to humor me just once more. Can we please go over what it's going to be like?"

Dennis shook his head. "I'm no longer your best source of information, boss. You should talk to Wilkes and

Gomez. They've actually been out there. I'm afraid they're a much better source than I can be at this point."

Grabowski grimaced. "OK," he began. "Allow me to rephrase this." He continued almost kindly. "The information I can get from those two men is *tactical* in nature. It allows me to do some effective short-term planning. What I'm looking for now is *strategic* information. Yes, we have to get through the day-to-day. *But*: without a long range plan in place, the day-to-day may never amount to anything more than just that. Do you understand, son?"

Dennis took a huge chance. "You miss them, don't you General?"

For a split second intense pain flickered behind Grabowski's eyes. Instantly he replaced it with the concrete hard expression that was the only face the survivors would remember. "I asked you a question and I expect an answer," he said harshly.

Dennis gave up. "Life will," he said.

"What the hell does that mean?" asked an irate Grabowski.

"Just a saying I used to have in my office," responded Dennis. "Historically there is nothing that has ever happened on this planet that has managed to wipe out life. So even if we don't make it, *something* will. LIFE will go on — with us or without us."

"That doesn't exactly answer my question," he snapped.

"Alright," sighed Schweigert. "Let's get this over with. Why don't we get Wilkes in here too so we can have as many people in on the plan as possible?"

Grabowski nodded. "Not a bad idea," he responded. "I'll send for him." As he walked out in search of a runner, he stopped and looked over his shoulder. With more than a trace of sadness he said, "Of course I miss them Dennis. I'm going to miss them every single moment of my miserable existence. But to honor their memory, I am going to use every single resource I have available to me to guarantee the survival of our species. That means your brains and experience, Coffey's baby, and whatever else I can think of. 'LIFE might' but you can make damned sure that 'Grabowski WILL.'"

Karl Roscoe

It was finally time. The appointed day of departure had come. The seven hundred some-odd survivors gathered near the closed door with a mixture of anticipation, fear, remorse and unbridled excitement. Their adventure was just beginning. Each took with him some memento or two that they could easily carry. Grabowski had chosen a sidearm; a nine-millimeter pistol like the one he had carried throughout his career. Jack Wilkes raised an eyebrow when he saw Grabowski strap it on. The only answer was a slight shrug. Wilkes shook his head with a small smile and continued his preparations. Then, without any formal presentation, Grabowski ordered the door opened and he stepped into the tunnel.

It was horrific. The bodies they'd placed outside had

warmed just enough to begin decomposing. The smell alone was staggering. Seeing those that they had lived with, laughed with and, for some, loved, caused a tightening in their gut and a gagging in their throats. But they had been through worse. And worse yet was waiting for them out there. Like Grabowski had taught them, they steeled their nerves and marched past the bodies, concentrating on the light coming from the end of the tunnel.

Grabowski led them out over toward the fence where they all gathered for a moment. Everyone took a deep breath when they exited the tunnel, hoping to clear the stench of rotting flesh from their nostrils. It was not to be. If Hell itself had a smell, it was this that greeted them on the outside. Harsh, pungent, bitter and acrid, it burned their olfactories. Grabowski looked them all over as they gathered in the hostile air. He then looked at the sky. It was blue. Far above them was a circle of the free, blue sky they had not seen in more than two years. Below this arc there ran menacing brown clouds, laced with white edges. And over the mountains themselves lay a gray/brown mist, the last remnants of the cataclysm. "Let's go," he grunted and began the long hike down Cheyenne Mountain Road.

Along the way they found acre-sized patches of snow waiting to melt. The temperature had made it up to the high forties but, between the brisk wind and the snow patches, it was quite chilly. They marched forward, eyes on the horizon. There was almost no chatter. Each understood that the business of survival was now their only concern. So, with the likeness of combat-hardened veterans, they followed their leader down the road towards the city of Colorado Springs.

About a third of the way down, they saw it. A lone figure was walking up the hill to meet them. There was a low buzz among the seven hundred. Grabowski continued on as if there were nothing at all odd in this occurrence. As they approached they began to make out some features on the stranger. He or she was wearing a blanket as a cloak. They couldn't decide on gender because the figure was wearing a gas mask. Slowly the figure and the group came together near a large patch of icy snow. They all stopped. A muffled voice came from the mask.

"I've been waiting quite some time," it said.

Grabowski declined to answer.

"I thought you might need some help," the muffled voice continued.

"I don't believe we're going to require your help," responded Grabowski. "We're doing quite well." This caused another stir among the survivors.

The figure reached up and tugged the mask over the top of his head. "You sure about that, General?" grinned a gaunt but otherwise very much alive Mark Zorbas. An electric buzz circulated through the crowd. Alexis covered Nadja protectively while Mr. Palmer stepped in front of her, as if to block any view.

"Positive. Now step aside." There was no denying

the authority in Grabowski's tone.

"Not so fast, General. Where is everybody? I remember there being a whole lot more folks than this when I left." The grin remained frozen on his face.

There was no answer to his question. The crowd's excitement at finding another survivor had transformed into pure malice at discovering the man's identity.

"Where's my girl?" Mark shouted, looking on tiptoes at the crowd. "I've been pretty lonely. Sure could use some company!"

"You finished?" asked Grabowski. "We've got work to do."

"Hell, I'm just getting started!" chirped Mark. "I expect there's a whole bunch of things you need to know about living out here and I'm the only one who knows 'em."

"Like I said, we'll do just fine. Without you."

"I don't think you get it, Grabowski," said Zorbas haughtily. "Things are a little different out here." Opening his arms wide, he said, "See, I'm the only one out here who knows about how to stay alive. That puts you all in a bit of a pinch." Waving his hands happily, he paced—almost danced—as he spoke. "Now, I believe that you'll get used to doing things my way after a while. You've proven to be a very adaptable bunch." His grin hardened. He appeared to be enjoying this moment immensely. His eyes belied the lightness of his step, however. They were bitter and callous.

"I disagree," reiterated Grabowski. "Now step aside.

We have things to do."

"Make me," said Mark, moving threateningly toward him.

Grabowski smoothly slid a practiced hand toward the hilt of his pistol. With one fluid motion, he drew and fired directly into Mark Zorbas' chest. As Mark's eyes widened with disbelief, Grabowski fired again. Mark dropped to his knees, blood spilling over the two hands he now had clutched to his chest. Grabowski holstered his weapon and, grunting a "Let's go," at his followers, began the march down the mountain road once more. One by one they followed him. Gurgling through the blood, Mark pitched over on one side. In single file they walked past the man dying there in the snow, deep crimson clashing with the bright white. One by one they stepped past him or over him. They didn't look at him. They only looked out over the city. Zorbas was their past. The city was their future. Reaching out with a blood-soaked hand, he begged for help. He would die there, more alone than he had been in the year since he had been cast out. Long before the last survivor had passed him, Mark Zorbas had breathed his last breath. And they kept marching, stone faced, into the very uncertain future of the human race.

Afterward

I have been asked by virtually everyone who has proofed this book: "Is this real? Could this really happen?" The simple and direct answer is "Yes." Yes, Cheyenne Mountain Air Force Base is a real place. Yes, it was decommissioned and put into "warm storage." Yes, Yellowstone is the largest known caldera, and yes, it is overdue to erupt. Finally, yes, a killer asteroid could still hit the Earth with little or no warning. As of September of 2007, almost 5000 Near Earth Objects (NEO's) have been discovered and catalogued by NASA's Near Earth Object Program; 722 of them are considered to be "large." Let's just say that we've been living lucky so far.

There you have it! I hope you've had as much fun with this story as I have. Incidentally, I don't know what happens to them. Humans are a resilient bunch. We've beaten some pretty remarkable odds in the past—maybe that'll continue. And they're not out there alone. I've given them the most powerful of human survival tools. They've got Hope. And the future. Thanks for coming with me on this trip!
Karl

Karl Roscoe earned his Bachelor's Degree in English Literature in 1984 at the University of Massachusetts, Amherst. He spent almost 19 years as a pilot with the Air Force. Following a short stint in the garbage industry and a few other adventures, he has returned to his first love; writing. Karl currently lives in Colorado with his family. He still enjoys flying and can be found in an airplane whenever his schedule permits.

www.karlroscoebooks.info